"Holly..."

Matt rasped her name as he cupped his palms against her cheeks and angled his head for a deeper kiss.

A rumble of satisfaction issued from his throat when Holly swept her tongue into his mouth to duel with his.

The heavy beat that her heart had pounded as they danced now thundered, shaking her to the core. Her skin flushed hot, and a coil of desire tightened inside her.

She tasted the cinnamon and cloves of the spiced cider on his lips and longed to savor Matt's kiss for hours.

But the jarring ring of her phone jangled from the kitchen.

She didn't want to move, didn't want to talk to anyone. She wanted only to step back into Matt's arms and continue the heavenly kiss.

Dear Reader,

I *love* Christmas! As soon as the first cool nip hits the air in the autumn, I start counting down the days until the Christmas season when I can decorate, bake, sing carols, shop, send cards and watch all the beloved Christmas movie classics. So what could be better than writing a Christmas book? Maybe the chance to write a Christmas book that I'd had swimming around in my head for years *and* kick off a new trilogy of stories about three sisters' perilous journeys to the altar.

The Christmas Stranger is the first book in my new miniseries, THE BANCROFT BRIDES, in which each of the Bancroft sisters (Paige, Holly and Zoey) finds danger and adventure before they walk down the aisle to happily ever after. And fate has a few surprises in store regarding their Mr. Rights!

Set during the Christmas season in the beautiful Smoky Mountains of North Carolina, *The Christmas Stranger* is a story of my heart. I hope you will love Matt and Holly's emotional story as much as I did. Then watch for Paige's and Zoey's exciting stories coming in 2010!

Let me be the first this year to wish you a merry Christmas!

Happy reading,

Beth Cornelison

BETH CORNELISON

The Christmas Stranger

Silhouette®

Romantic

SUSPENSE

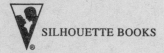

SILHOUETTE BOOKS

Recycling programs
for this product may
not exist in your area.

ISBN-13: 978-0-373-27651-6

THE CHRISTMAS STRANGER

Printed in U.S.A.

Books by Beth Cornelison

Silhouette Romantic Suspense

BETH CORNELISON

started writing stories as a child when she penned a tale about the adventures of her cat, Ajax. A Georgia native, she received her bachelor's degree in public relations from the University of Georgia. After working in public relations for a little more than a year, she moved with her husband to Louisiana, where she decided to pursue her love of writing fiction.

Since that first time, Beth has written many more stories of adventure and romantic suspense and has won numerous honors for her work, including a coveted Golden Heart award for romantic suspense from Romance Writers of America. She is active on the board of directors for the North Louisiana Storytellers and Authors of Romance (NOLA STARS) and loves reading, traveling, Peanuts' Snoopy and spending downtime with her family.

She writes from her home in Louisiana, where she lives with her husband, one son and two cats who think they are people. Beth loves to hear from her readers. You can write to her at P.O. Box 5418, Bossier City, LA 71171, or visit her Web site at www.bethcornelison.com.

In memory of my grandmother Alice Miles.
I miss you and think of you often.

North Carolina holds a special place
in my heart because of you.

Chapter 1

Ryan's killer was most likely a vagrant.

With her brother-in-law's assessment echoing in her head, Holly Bancroft Cole suppressed a shiver. Rubbing her arms, she cast an appraising glance around the Halloween party at the Community Aid Center in Morgan Hollow, North Carolina.

New faces dotted the crowd. But were any of them killers?

A loud cheer turned her attention to the festivities. The center's volunteers had all dressed up in goofy, creative and occasionally creepy costumes to entertain the city's homeless and underprivileged children. At the moment, two clowns led the kids on a wild scavenger hunt for candy, while Holly, wearing her bridal gown, oversaw the refreshments. The children's parents hovered along the walls, as well as a few men who were regulars at the donated clothing room or the center's soup kitchen. While the party was billed as a children's Halloween bash, no one had been turned away.

Flipping back her bridal veil for a better view, Holly

scanned the unshaven, bedraggled faces of the vagrants who'd gathered this Friday for free hot cider, entertainment and a warm place to pass the chilly October afternoon. Could one of these men have killed Ryan for his watch, wallet and Reeboks?

Apprehension and suspicion crawled up her spine.

Little evidence had been collected at the crime scene just over a year ago when her husband had been murdered and robbed. The local police, including her brother-in-law Robert, called Ryan's death a tragic, random attack. Robert held out little hope that Ryan's killer would ever be caught.

But Robert's gloomy outlook didn't sit well for Holly. She wanted resolution to the many mysteries concerning Ryan's attack. She wanted justice. And she needed closure. While she'd come to grips with Ryan's death and had begun picking up the pieces of her shattered life, she hated all the blanks in the account of what happened the night Ryan was killed.

Maybe the police wouldn't ever have enough evidence to bring a suspect to trial, as Robert projected. But any tiny shred of understanding would go a long way in settling the nagging questions she had.

"You know, you should have smeared some blood on your face or worn a scary mask."

Carol Hamburg's comment yanked Holly from her morose thoughts.

"That wedding dress is great, but you could have come as the Bride of Frankenstein or something."

Tucking a stray wisp of her blond hair behind her ear, Holly shrugged as she faced the Community Aid Center's petite director. "I'd considered fake blood, but I really didn't want to risk getting makeup on the dress. I wore this gown when I married Ryan, and I've worn it every year since for Halloween. It's a tradition."

"Really? How'd that get started?"

Holly smiled wistfully. "After our wedding, I complained to Ryan about how much the dress cost, to be worn only once. So, frugal and practical man that he was, he dared me to use it every Halloween as my costume." She paused and sighed. "I almost didn't put it on today. But I'm glad I did. It makes me feel closer to him."

Carol blinked her surprise. "I'm just jealous you're still the same size you were when you got married."

Before Holly could reply, a loud cry rose over the chatter in the room. She and Carol exchanged a concerned look before moving together in the direction of the commotion. The crowd of curious children, startled mothers and homeless men shrank away from a little boy in superhero pajamas lying on the floor unconscious.

His lips were blue.

Icy horror washed through Holly in concentric waves as the reality of what was happening sank over her.

"Call 9-1-1!" she shouted to Carol as she dashed to the boy's side and dropped to her knees.

"He's not breathing!" the child's mother screamed. The woman dragged the child up by the arms and began pounding on his back.

"Don't do that!" One of the unshaven men separated from the others and rushed forward. He placed a hand on the frightened mother's shoulder and met her eyes. "Let me have him."

The woman hesitated only a second before relinquishing her son to the dark-haired man. "Please! Save him!"

"I'll do my best," he replied, his voice deep and calm. He gently laid the boy back on the floor. After feeling for a pulse in the boy's neck, he leaned close to listen and look for signs of breathing.

Glancing at Holly, he said, "Watch his chest for me. Tell me if it rises."

Nodding, Holly scooted back to give the man room to work as he angled the boy's head and blew two breaths in the boy's mouth.

"Anything?"

Holly shook her head. "I didn't see it move."

The man frowned. "Something's obstructing the airway."

Quickly he moved to straddle the boy's legs and stacked his hands on the child's abdomen. "Come on, sport. Stay with me," he mumbled as he gave five sharp upward thrusts with his palms. Crawling to the boy's side, the dark-haired man did a visual check of the boy's mouth then swept his finger inside. With a deep sigh of relief, he withdrew a piece of hard candy and tossed it aside.

But the boy didn't move, didn't draw a breath.

Pressing his lips in a taut line, the man glanced up and drilled a hard glare at Holly. His sky-blue eyes were clear and intense. "You, the bride. Help me."

Holly blinked, rallying from her fear-based daze. "How?"

"Give him two full breaths in his mouth, five seconds apart, every time I say *now*."

She nodded her understanding and scrambled closer as the man started chest compressions. Adrenaline spiked her pulse as she watched the man working to save the young boy.

"Now." His clear blue eyes met hers, echoing his command.

Holly bent low and covered the boy's mouth with hers. Blew. Counted five and blew again.

"Good. Just like that." Jerking a nod, he resumed compressions.

Holly studied the boy now. His lips had regained a bit of their color, but he remained unconscious. She glanced up at his panicked and crying mother. "He's going to be okay. I promise."

Why she was so certain, she couldn't say. It was risky to assure the mother when she didn't truly know how this rescue effort would go. But a strange assurance and confidence in the man working on the little boy flowed through her, calming her own frayed nerves.

Holly moved her gaze to Carol, who held a cell phone to her ear. With a look, Holly asked for an update.

"An ambulance is on its way. The operator is still on the line," Carol said softly.

"Now."

Holly met the man's eyes briefly before dipping her head to give another breath. Count five. Breath.

As she raised her head from the last puff, the boy coughed, gasped in air.

"Tommy!" his mother cried and tried to hug him.

"Give me a minute," the boy's rescuer instructed, sidling between the mother and child. Again he checked the boy's pulse, lifted his eyelids to check his pupils, examined the child's fingernails. "Tommy, can you hear me? Can you talk?"

"I want Mommy," the boy whimpered.

The man smiled, flashing a set of perfect white teeth as he backed up. "She's right here, sport."

Holly dropped back on her heels, her muscles going limp with relief. She stared at the man who'd saved the boy, mulling the inconsistencies in his appearance. While she knew better than to judge anyone by how they looked, little about this man fit the profile of the average homeless client who came to the Community Aid Center. Though his cheeks and chin were covered in a few days' growth of beard like many of the other men the center served, his hair was much cleaner, his beard shorter and his skin healthier. In fact, despite needing a shave and a haircut, the square cut of the man's jaw, sharp angles of the man's cheeks and straight nose gave him an ironically patrician appearance.

"Thank you," she said, laying a hand on his arm. He turned from watching the mother hug her son. "You saved his life."

Again his bright blue eyes burrowed deep with their cool intensity, stirring an odd swirling in her belly. "No. *We* did. Together. Thank *you.*"

Holly shook her head. "I didn't—"

He wrapped a large hand around hers, and at his touch, the rest of her reply caught in her throat. A warm ripple of sensation skimmed over her. "Yes, you did."

She dropped her gaze to his tanned hand and wet her lips. "Really, you're the one who—" Again her words stalled as she focused on the watch peeking out from under the sleeve of his flannel shirt.

She knew that watch, hadn't seen that watch since the last morning Ryan left for work. That watch had been stolen from her husband the day he'd been attacked, *murdered* in an abandoned church not far from the Community Aid Center.

Gasping, she jerked a startled frown up to the man as her brother-in-law's words reverberated in her head.

Ryan's killer was most likely a vagrant.

Matt Rankin knew that look well. Disgust. Accusation. Contempt.

The exhilaration of having saved the choking boy evaporated under the icy glare from the center volunteer. When he touched her arm, the beautiful blonde bride who'd helped him resuscitate the boy gaped at his hand, her joy and admiration morphing suddenly into something ugly and cold.

"Where did you get that watch?" she demanded, her tone clipped and accusing. As if he had no right to own something of value.

And maybe he didn't. Maybe he should have sold the watch months ago to help pay for food, his rent, his child support. But he couldn't bring himself to part with the last thing he owned that Jill had given him.

He tamped down the swirl of emotions that still ravaged him when he thought of Jill's death and the terrible repercussions that followed. Keeping his tone even, he met the woman's hard green-eyed stare. "It was a Christmas gift from my wife a few years ago."

"Your wife?" She narrowed her eyes skeptically, as if being down on your luck and scrimping to make even a scant income meant you could never have had a wife and children, a home and career. A life to be proud of.

"Yes, my wife." Matt sighed. He didn't have much to be

proud of now, and he couldn't really blame the woman for her snap judgment. In her position, he might think much the same. But the past few months had taught him how close every person was to living on the street.

His golden life had suffered a chain reaction of tragic blows and shattered.

An ambulance arrived, and the crowd of spectators cleared a path as the rescue workers huddled around the boy and his mother, checking the child's vital signs.

Matt inhaled deeply, and looking back at the blonde woman, he pushed to his feet.

He dusted his hands off, then extended one to help the bride to her feet.

She glanced at his proffered hand, hesitated, then let him pull her from the floor.

"I'm sorry. I just... My husband had a watch like that one stolen, and—"

"You thought I'd stolen this one."

She turned away guiltily. "It just startled me to see it. Your watch is just like Ryan's and—" She huffed and smoothed a hand over the skirt of her wedding dress costume. "Never mind." She backed away one step, then forced a tight smile. "Thank you...for helping with Tommy. You saved his life." Her delicate brow furrowed, and she tipped her head. "How...how did you know what to do?"

"Anyone can learn CPR and the Heimlich maneuver. They are valuable skills to have." Yes, he was being evasive, cryptic, not fully forthcoming. But he didn't feel like explaining the whole sordid story of his ignoble downfall—which he'd inevitably have to. When he mentioned his medical degree, his career, the question always followed.

How did a successful doctor end up scavenging a meal from a soup kitchen on Halloween?

"Well, thank you. You saved the day." Her smile was brighter now, more genuine.

Matt's gut kicked. Her smile transformed her already beautiful face to nothing short of breathtaking. Not for the first time, his own ragged appearance left him feeling awkward and embarrassed. He nodded to the woman and turned to make his way through the crowd. He needed air, and the small room at the Community Aid Center had begun feeling cramped, stuffy.

As he stepped out of the building, the crisp autumn breeze nipped at his lungs and bit his cheeks with a sobering reminder that winter was mere weeks away. If he didn't want to freeze at night, he'd have to continue renting his ramshackle room at the Woodgate Inn. Which, in turn, meant he'd have to find a new source of income.

The irony of his situation appalled him. He had a medical degree, had graduated top of his class. But thanks to his appearance, his lack of transportation or a permanent address, he couldn't find a job that paid enough to make his child support payments and also get ahead. The tanked economy didn't help, either. The few available jobs were grabbed up by mill workers who'd been laid off, or clean-cut, white-collar men taking second jobs to cover their mortgages.

Pulling his collar up against the cold wind blowing off the slopes of the North Carolina Smoky Mountains, Matt squared his shoulders and headed down the street. He was through feeling sorry for himself, finished wallowing in his pain and failure.

He wouldn't let the tragic turn of fate defeat him. He had to rebuild his life. For his kids.

He'd pull through this black period somehow and get back on his feet. He wouldn't quit—even if everyone he loved had quit on him.

Tommy's choking had rattled Holly, and seeing the watch, so much like Ryan's, on the man at the center had destroyed her interest in revelry. After making sure Tommy would be all right, Holly had sneaked away from the Halloween party and headed to her truck.

She'd already been giving a few hours each month to the Community Aid Center when Ryan was killed. Knowing one of the people she helped at the center could be responsible for the attack on her husband disturbed Holly deeply. She'd almost quit.

But the evil actions of one person didn't negate the good she was doing or the needs of the children she met at the center. Besides, what if she heard something through her volunteer work that could help the police catch Ryan's killer?

Over the past several months, she'd learned more about the homeless than she'd ever imagined. And many of her conceptions of who the homeless were and why they were on the streets had been blown out of the water. Many of the people she had helped had high school diplomas or professional skills, but medical bills to treat an illness had depleted their bank account. Or they'd been laid off a job and couldn't pay their rent. Or they'd fled an abusive situation and had nowhere to go.

A heartbreaking number of the center's clients were single mothers, struggling to survive and feed their kids. As an elementary school teacher, Holly loved kids, and the needs of the homeless children touched her heart the most. Every child deserved a safe home and a roof over his or her head.

Once she'd reached her Tacoma, she'd decided a brief walk to enjoy the October afternoon and clear her head was in order. She'd left the veil and detachable long skirt from her wedding dress on the front seat and put on a long cardigan over the travel suit portion of the gown.

Now she stood in front of the old abandoned church where Ryan had been killed and realized the church had always been her destination. Before his death, Ryan had driven her by the structure and joked that they should buy it and restore it, as they were doing with the rambling old farmhouse they'd bought outside of town. Holly had only scowled at him. "One never-ending, money-pit renovation project at a time, please!"

But Holly had been fascinated by the old church, the beautiful architecture and broken stained glass. The church had been a true treasure, lost to neglect and the elements. Since it was so close to the Community Aid Center, she had walked past the old church many times after she volunteered. She'd made the trip a sort of pilgrimage, a time to remember Ryan and renew her oath to find some truths and give herself closure.

Today, the familiar questions seemed all the more relentless. Why had Ryan been in the old church to begin with? Who had he come across in the abandoned building, and why did that someone bash him on the head, killing him?

Holly noticed white paper tacked to the front door and climbed over the yellow caution tape to read what had been posted on the church door.

Warning! Building Condemned—No trespassing! This building scheduled to be demolished November 1, 8:00 a.m.

Holly's heart squeezed in disappointment. Demolished? The church might be old and unused, but the architecture was beautiful, and the history attached to the old church was priceless. Why hadn't the Historical Society stepped in years ago to preserve the church? She hated to think of the loss to the community.

And what about the investigation into Ryan's murder? If they tore down the building, any remaining clues would be lost forever.

Not that any clues remained. Robert had told her that he and the other officers with Morgan Hollow's tiny police force had been through the crime scene multiple times and found precious little evidence to explain Ryan's death.

Holly bit her lip, grieved that tomorrow the church would be gone. An overwhelming need seized Holly to go inside the church one last time, see the room where Ryan had died, look once more for something, *anything* that could explain his death.

Some enterprising hooligan had smashed the padlock fastening the chain through the door handles. So much for security. Clearly she wasn't the only person interested in the old church. Drawing a deep breath and ignoring the warning not to trespass, she pulled the front door open and crept inside.

She'd only been inside the church once before, the week after Ryan died, while she'd still been lost in a blinding blizzard of emotions. Though she had visited the property regularly, she knew venturing inside the condemned building was dangerous. Today, that risk didn't matter to her. The compelling need to feel close to Ryan, search the premises for herself and say a last goodbye urged her forward. This exploration of the old church might be the closest thing she'd ever have to the closure she craved so desperately.

Cobwebs and dust decorated the walls and broken furnishings with an eerie ambience which any host of a Halloween party would envy. Taking baby steps into the shadowed foyer, Holly headed for the staircase. She grasped the wobbly banister, and the steps creaked as she slowly climbed toward the second floor.

Halfway to the top, a step gave way beneath her weight. Her foot disappeared through the rotted wood. She toppled off balance.

Gasping, Holly clutched the shaky railing to right herself. She paused long enough to suck in a calming breath and eye the last few steps warily. She considered her options, but the need to see the upstairs room where Ryan had died compelled her to continue.

Inching closer to the wall, where she hoped the steps had more support, she crept up the last few stairs. Her heart stuck in her throat. The hallway on the upper floor loomed in the shadows, the darkness broken only where watery daylight seeped through open doors. Dust motes swam in those pools of gray light, and Holly focused on the bright spots instead of the darkness. She paused at the first door on the left. The room where Ryan's body had been found.

Standing in the doorway, Holly gazed into the empty room. Paint peeled from the molding. A gaping hole, where a window had once resided, marred the outside wall. That window, a round piece of stained glass, rested on the floor, propped in a corner.

The room was so still, so quiet—except for her own labored breathing, the pounding pulse in her ears and the occasional coo of a mourning dove from the evergreen tree outside. As a cloud moved away from the afternoon sun, a golden beam poured in through the open hole in the wall and spilled across the floor. The sun lit the stained glass, bringing life to the arrangement of colors.

In the center of the window, a white dove took flight, while all around the bird a dazzling jumble of colors created a brilliant backdrop.

"Wow," she murmured, stunned by the gorgeous find in the otherwise lonely and dreary old church. Holly stepped farther into the room and squatted in front of the stained glass for a better look. Upon closer examination she discovered the glass piece, unlike the many other windows in the church, was intact. The small window was in almost perfect condition. A bit of cleaning and a new setting would salvage it, and a tiny piece of history would survive.

Holly's pulse picked up as she formed her plan. If she could somehow get the stained glass to her truck, she could incorporate the window in the ongoing renovations at the farmhouse.

She tried to lift the glass. Her muscles strained, and she got it off the floor...but getting the heavy, fragile window down the steps and to her truck would be a challenge. Especially since she still wore her wedding travel suit. She casually put it back.

If she didn't save the window, it would be destroyed in the

morning when the wrecking crew arrived. She stood and chewed her lip, considering her options.

She paced toward the door, out to the hall, glancing about for something she could put the glass on to slide it across the floor. Or use as leverage. Or…

As she mulled her options, her thoughts darted in a different direction.

Ryan.

He'd have loved this stained glass. What if—

"Is *this* what you were doing here, Ry—?" Something brushed against Holly's leg, and she froze.

A dark streak moved in the edge of her vision. Her breath hung in her lungs. She turned slowly, her gaze searching the dim room.

And spotted a scruffy, thin cat staring back at her uneasily. With a low warning meow, the cat scampered from the shadows into the next room. Holly followed the cat, which made its way to a pile of rags heaped in the corner. The cat's arrival started a chorus of high, thin mewls.

Holly released a sigh, while the stray mother cat tended her kittens. Pulling her lips in a half smile, she edged closer. "Hey, little mama, I won't hurt you or your babies."

The cat protested with an unhappy meow and crouched low beside her nest of five kittens. The babies were tiny, their eyes barely open.

Holly's heart fisted. They'd be killed when the wrecking ball came to raze the old church tomorrow. She had to do something, but the mother cat looked none too pleased to have someone poking around near her brood.

"Easy there, mama. I won't hurt—"

The scuff of feet cut Holly off.

A long, wide shadow fell over her, and a chill settled in her bones. Gasping, she whirled around.

A tall man with shoulders that filled the doorway blocked her only exit. His face was hidden in shadow. When he spoke, his voice was deep and dark. "What are you doing?"

Staring at the disheveled man who had her cornered in the dark room, Holly immediately conjured Robert's theory.

Ryan's killer was most likely a vagrant.

Chapter 2

Holly shoved to her feet, tried to answer.

Her voice stuck in her throat.

"Didn't you see the sign? This place has been condemned. It's dangerous." The man stepped farther into the room, moving out of the shadow that had obscured his face.

Holly recognized the dark-haired man with piercing blue eyes who'd saved Tommy's life, then disappeared from the Halloween party without a word.

Her scampering pulse calmed a bit, but she kept a wary distance. As he moved closer, she edged away. "I…just wanted…to have a last look. This church is important to me, and…I wanted…needed…"

She huffed a sigh. How did she explain about Ryan's murder, the questions that needed answers, the closeness she felt to Ryan here? *Why* should she explain?

She straightened her spine and leveled her shoulders. "Never mind my reasons. I knew the risks and weighed them."

He gave a negligent shrug. "All right."

His gaze shifted to the pile of rags where the kittens squeaked and fussed.

Holly cleared her throat. "Why are you here?"

His cool, clear eyes found hers again. "I saw you go in and followed you."

A prickle of apprehension crawled through her. "Why?"

"Like I said, the place is condemned. It could be dangerous. I didn't want you breaking a leg and being stuck in here alone."

She blinked at him, stunned. "Really?"

He angled his head and tugged up a corner of his mouth. "Really."

Holly's gaze lingered on his lips, visible despite the growth of several days' beard. His lips were full, soft-looking…sexy. She shifted her feet, uncomfortable with the track of her thoughts. This man was a vagrant. Rumpled, unshaven, dirty. How could she find anything about him appealing?

Yet she remembered how, back at the community center, his blue eyes and calming touch had stirred a warmth in her belly. She sensed something different about him and puzzled over the source of that intuition.

He nodded to the nest of kittens. "Is this why you came in here? Did you know they were here?"

Holly wiped sweaty palms on her dress, then grimaced. She'd left dirty smears on the skirt. "No. But now that I've found them, I can't leave them to die in the demolition tomorrow."

"No. I reckon we can't."

She raised her chin. "We?"

"I'm at your disposal if you want my help." When she hesitated, he stuck his hand out. "We met earlier but didn't introduce ourselves. I'm Matt."

She took his hand, trembling when his long fingers closed warmly around hers. "Holly." She thought of the stained glass in the next room and held her breath. "If you're serious about helping, there is something…"

He tipped his head. "Yeah?"

When she didn't answer for a few seconds, he crouched by the kittens. The mother cat hissed and ran.

"Mom's gonna be hard to catch. Harder to transport." He picked up a kitten and stroked it with a finger. "They look pretty healthy. Too young to be without mom though. We'll have to wrangle her to go with the babies, somehow."

Holly appraised Matt more closely. Could she trust him?

His clothes, though well-worn, somewhat dirty and wrinkled, had been high quality when new. She recognized the name brand logo on his shirt pocket and designer cut of his slacks. Turning this incongruity over in her mind, she wondered where he'd gotten the expensive clothes. When he'd smiled, she'd noticed how white and straight his teeth were. Another anomaly among the men typically served at the Community Aid Center. So who was he? What was his story?

Trusting her gut, she squatted next to him and gently patted one of the squirming kittens. "I found a stained-glass window in the next room I want to save, too. It's pretty heavy, but maybe between the two of us, we could get it to my truck."

He met her gaze and nodded. "Sure, let's have a look."

Holly showed him the stained glass and stood back as he hefted it into his arms with little effort. "Lead the way."

Taking the steps carefully, keeping near the wall, she led him outside and down the street to her truck. He rested the stained glass on the tailgate while she rearranged some painting supplies in the bed to make room for the window.

"I'm remodeling my farmhouse, and this glass would be perfect in the entry foyer over the door."

"It *is* beautiful," he agreed, settling it on the drop cloth she'd spread out. He dusted his hands and gave her a hard look. "You have someone at your house to help you unload it?"

Holly bit her bottom lip as she thought. "I can call one of my brothers-in-law to come over, perhaps."

"What about your husband?"

Holly's heartbeat stumbled, and she swallowed hard before she answered. "He died last year."

Matt's face darkened as his eyebrows drew together. "I'm so sorry. I lost my wife a few years ago myself. I know how hard it can be."

"I'm sorry for you, too." Her gaze flicked to the watch on his wrist that he'd told her was from his wife. The timepiece would have been an expensive gift. Had Matt come from a wealthy family? He certainly spoke like an educated man. If so, how had he suffered such a reversal of fortune?

"Now, about those kittens…" Matt scrubbed a hand on his chin, his beard making a scratching sound that danced down Holly's spine with a pleasant shiver.

Holly reached into the truck bed and dumped paint brushes out of a small box. "We can put the babies in here. But the mother won't come willingly."

"Exactly. I was thinking we could wrap her up in a towel or one of those rags upstairs. Wrap her tightly like a mummy. It won't hurt her, but she won't be able to struggle and scratch us."

Us. He was using the plural pronoun again.

She frowned. "Matt, I—"

He held up a hand. "I know what you're thinking, but…you can't drive and subdue a frightened cat at the same time. If you're willing to drive me back into town tonight, I'll put my arms on the line with the scared feline and help you unload the window at your house."

Holly stared at him, debating his argument, his offer. "What's in it for you? Why would you do that for me?"

His eyes widened, and he shook his head. "Who said there was anything in it for me? Aren't you a little tired of the selfish attitude society has come to? What happened to being a good neighbor and helping out for the sake of being nice?"

Holly opened her mouth, but no sound came out. Matt seemed too good to be true. Already today he'd saved a boy's life without sticking around for the accolades. If she were to believe him, he'd been worried for her safety and come into the abandoned church to make sure she was all right.

Narrowing a skeptical look on him, she pinched his arm. "Are you for real?"

He rubbed the offended spot. "Yeah, and that hurt."

Holly crossed her arms over her chest. "So you're not like a guardian angel or something?"

"Afraid not." He flashed his white smile, a dimple pocking one cheek and his blue eyes twinkling in the afternoon sun.

Holly's pulse fluttered.

He was undeniably attractive, even with his rumpled clothes and scraggly beard. His eyes were stone-cold sober, and she didn't smell any alcohol around him. He just didn't fit any of the stereotypes for vagrants she'd learned over the years.

She shook her head. "You're not like most of the men that come to the Community Aid Center for help."

"I hope that's a good thing." Sobering his expression, he said, "I understand your concern, though. We just met. You don't know if you can trust me. The whole safety issue, right?"

She lifted her chin. "A girl has to be careful."

"You're right." He nodded and stroked his chin again. "You could pat me down to check for weapons." He raised his arms and gave a devilish wink. "But I'm not carrying."

She returned a grin. "Or I could call my brother-in-law, the cop, to run your name through their computer and get the lowdown on you."

His smile faltered, and Holly experienced her first real misgivings. Why did mention of the police bother him? She'd been bluffing, but Matt's reaction spurred her to dig out her cell phone.

Matt sighed and jammed his hands in his pockets. "Go ahead…if it will put your mind at rest."

Holly dialed Robert's cell and wasted no time with small talk. "Can you check a name out for me? Matt…" She looked to Matt, lifting her hand to invite him to fill in the missing last name.

"Rankin."

"Rankin. Matt Rankin. He have a record?"

"Is this for the Center?" Robert asked.

"Uh...yeah," she lied. "Sorta," she added to ease her conscience.

"Just a minute." She heard the click of computer keys and a silent pause. "Nope, no arrests, but—"

"But?"

More clicking keys.

"Ah. He received unemployment checks at one point, so he is in the system. I show a mailing address at the Woodgate Inn. That help?"

"Yes, thank you, Robert."

Unemployment checks could mean Matt was one of the workers laid off when the local paper mill shut down production, and the Woodgate Inn was low-cost, bare-bones housing near the Community Aid Center. That much of Matt's story fit.

"Wanna tell me what this is about?" Robert asked.

"Not really. I'll call you later." She disconnected the call before her brother-in-law could protest.

Matt lifted an eyebrow, silently asking what she'd learned.

Holly shoved her phone back in her purse and shrugged. "Apparently Matt Rankin has no record."

He lifted a corner of his mouth, his smile guileless. "Then shall we catch a cat?"

"Stand back." Matt stood in Holly's barn, ready to release the mother cat from the wrapping of rags they'd used to secure and transport her to Holly's home in the country. They'd settled the kittens in a comfortable box-bed with a towel in a safe corner of the barn. Now it was Mama's turn to see her new home. "She's bound to be scared and confused. Who knows what she'll do."

Holly nodded and inched back as Matt lowered the bundled cat to the floor and began unwinding the rag-wrapping. Already the cat's nose, poking out of the rags, twitched and sniffed the fresh air, redolent with the scents of straw and fallen leaves. As the bindings around the cat's legs loosened, she wiggled and sprang free, leaving a gash on Matt's arm as she vaulted away and scurried out of the barn.

Holly's green eyes rounded with concern. Rushing to the door, she scanned the yard. "She ran under the front porch."

"She'll be fine. She just needs to calm down. I bet in a couple weeks, she'll be eating out of your hand." He examined the scratch on his arm and swiped the beading blood on his pants leg. "Speaking of which, do you have food?"

Holly pivoted on her toe and tucked a wisp of her silky blond hair behind her ear. The early evening sun bathed her in a golden light that made her hair shine and the white dress she wore glow with ethereal femininity. She'd asked if he was a guardian angel, but if he were a betting man, he'd wager *she* was the angel. She sure looked the part.

She blinked and fumbled as if his question surprised her. "Oh, well, I...of course. In fact, I, um...have chili cooking in the Crock-Pot."

He lowered his brow. "I'm not sure the cat will like anything spicy."

She tipped her head at an endearing angle. "The cat? I...was inviting you to have some dinner before I drove you back to town."

"Oh." Matt shifted his feet uneasily. Being on the receiving end of charity still rankled. But to survive the toughest months recently, he'd had to swallow his pride. "I wasn't asking for myself. I meant do you have cat food?"

Holly's cheeks flushed a delicate pink, and she wrapped her arms around her middle, chuckling awkwardly. "Sorry. I thought...but you are welcome to have some chili before you go back to town. I have plenty."

"I don't want to impose."

She waved off his demurral. "It's the least I can do."

Matt hesitated. A hot meal in the company of a beautiful woman did sound appealing. But…

He glanced down at his dirty clothes and grubby hands. He hated the slip in his hygiene of late. Without access to a washing machine or a working shower, he'd had to make concessions that made him cringe. He was hardly fit company for Holly in his disheveled and dingy state. His gut churned with disgust, frustration and shame. He hated where his life had ended up, but he had only to think of his children to know he'd make the same choices again if he were in the same position. His needs ranked a distant second to providing a secure, happy, healthy life for Palmer and Miles.

"I, um…" Staring down at his hands, he turned up his palms and ground his teeth together, swallowing the bitter taste that rose in his throat. Humble pie was not a sweet dish for a man who'd once been on top and had the world at his feet.

"You can use the shower off the guest room if you want before we eat."

He glanced up and found Holly watching him with a genuine openness and warmth.

"And I still have some of my husband's clothes that I think will fit you. You're welcome to them. They're not doing me any good collecting dust in my closet."

Matt held Holly's gaze, searched her face. If he'd seen even a hint of pity or hesitation in her expression, he'd have refused. He'd have hit the road.

He'd want to die on the spot.

But her smile was friendly and warm. Honest and unassuming.

"Okay." He jammed his hands in his pockets and returned a grateful smile. "You're very gracious."

"Maybe." Her grin brightened with a teasing glint. "Or maybe I'm tired of all the selfishness in society and want to be a good neighbor. Like you were for me."

A happiness Matt hadn't known in a long time bubbled up

from beneath the layers of guilt, frustration and humiliation. A burst of laughter erupted from him. "In that case, I accept. But let me unload the stained glass for you first."

She winked. "Deal."

He followed her back to her Tacoma, indulging in a leisurely glance at her slim, swaying hips as she crossed her leaf-strewn lawn.

Holly's matter-of-fact acceptance was a refreshing change from the condescending glares and judgmental comments he usually received from strangers. Her kindness and honesty stirred a hopeful warmth in his gut. Her simple beauty and girl-next-door smiles awoke a purely male response that heated his blood. And the hint of sadness that lurked in her eyes spoke to the man who'd seen his own share of tragedy and loss.

Matt wasn't gullible enough to believe in love at first sight, but something about Holly spoke to his soul, and he treasured the opportunity to get to know her better.

Even if he knew their current stations in life meant he had no future with her.

As she chopped a tomato for a salad later that evening, Holly heard the upstairs water cut off. Inhaling deeply, she stared down at the vegetable on her chopping board and worked to clear her mind of the sultry images of Matt in the shower that taunted her. After changing into jeans and a Snoopy T-shirt, she'd left towels, a disposable razor, clean clothes and a few toiletry items on the guest bed for Matt. While he showered, she'd taken his dirty clothes to wash.

Helping Matt felt good. Though she volunteered at the Community Aid Center a couple days a month, dishing up lunch to the masses and reading books to young children didn't seem as valuable a contribution as giving Matt a chance to clean up and have a hot meal. The personal connection made all the difference. She'd seen Matt be a friendly, helpful man and been compelled to respond in kind. Considering he had saved Tommy's life, a shower and supper were the least Matt deserved.

As Holly scraped the chopped tomato onto the salad, her phone rang.

"Hello?" She cradled the receiver between her shoulder and ear, while she started peeling carrots.

"Hey, sis! Happy Halloween!"

The youngest of the three Bancroft sisters, Zoey, sounded as bubbly and full of life as ever. Holly could well imagine Zoey decked out in some outrageous costume befitting her wild and rebellious personality. "Hey yourself. What's the plan for the Bancroft sisters down in Lagniappe this Halloween?"

"Well, *I'm* going to a party, but Paige's wimping out. I tell you, Hol, that stuffed shirt she's marrying is sucking all the fun outta our sister. She's trying to conform to some Stepford Wife mentality that he's brainwashed her with and never does anything without his approval. It's sick."

Given that Zoey was prone to hyperbole, Holly didn't let this report on their newly engaged older sister concern her. "I'm sure it's not as bad as all that."

"Oh, but it is! She spends *all* her time with Brent. I can barely get her on the phone anymore, because he's keeping her so busy with the most ridiculous wedding details. I mean, who really cares if she wears white stockings or tan? No one sees her legs under her gown anyway."

"Give her a break, Zoey. When I married Ryan, I wanted everything to be perfect, too. Remember?"

"But at least you spent time with your sisters before you let your husband drag you off to North Carolina."

Holly laughed. "You make it sound like Ryan brought me to Siberia."

"Might as well be. I miss not having you here in Lagniappe."

Holly sighed and experienced a tug of nostalgia for her family home in Louisiana. "I miss you, too, kiddo. Remember, the invite to come see me for Thanksgiving is still open."

"Thanks, but you know I don't plan that far in advance."

That was Zoey—the rebel, the party girl, living in the moment.

Holly sensed the change in Zoey's mood even before the familiar question came. "How are you doing, Holly?"

In other words, how was the poor widowed sister managing alone? Holly pinched the bridge of her nose and took the question in the spirit it was intended. Her family loved her and worried about her. Especially since Ryan's murder. They'd been surprised when she'd opted to stay in North Carolina after his death rather than return to her parents' home in Lagniappe. She may have grown up in Louisiana, but Morgan Hollow and the farmhouse she'd bought with Ryan were her home now.

"I'm fine, Zoey. Really." Holly heard footsteps on the stairs and added, "And I have company right now, so I need to go."

"You're ditching me, too?"

"Sorry. I'll call you later to hear all about that Halloween party. Meantime, try to cut Paige some slack. Okay?"

"Right." The resignation in Zoey's voice gave Holly pause. Was there more going on with her younger sister than feeling abandoned by Paige?

"Bye, sis. Love you." But Zoey had hung up and silence answered Holly. She replaced the receiver with a sigh and walked back to the chopping board.

"Do you have my clothes?"

Startled by the voice behind her, Holly fumbled the knife and nicked her finger. She set the blade down and turned. "I put them in the washing ma—"

The man standing in the door of her kitchen stole her breath, her thoughts, her balance. Reaching behind her, she caught the edge of the sink, wheezing, "Wow."

Wow was an understatement. Matt's piercing blue eyes, Colgate-perfect smile and broad shoulders had only been the tip of the proverbial iceberg. Holly gaped at the man who could have been an L.L. Bean model in another life.

Ryan's khaki slacks rode low on Matt's hips, and he'd combed back his damp, collar-length hair from his now clean-shaven face. His narrow feet were bare, and the crisp scent of soap wafted to her from where he stood.

Matt's brow furrowed. "Something wrong?"

"Uh, no. I…you…Wow. I barely recognize you!"

Matt smoothed a hand down the front of Ryan's old blue polo shirt. "Thanks for the clothes. You're sure you want to give them up?"

"They're not doing me any good in his closet. Someone should use them. Why not you?" She let her gaze take in the breath-stealing sight he made once more, then cleared her throat. "They seem to fit well."

He tugged at the waist of the slacks and nodded. "Darn close. Thanks." When he glanced up again, the vivid blue of his eyes, such a stark contrast to his dark hair and tanned skin, hit her with the force of a fist in the gut.

So bright, so clear, so piercing. *Yowza.*

His eyebrows lowered as he frowned. "Hey, you're bleeding."

"Huh?" She glanced down at her hands and saw the blood smeared on her finger. "Oh, that's nothing. I—"

He moved across the kitchen, his gait smooth and loose limbed. Taking her hand in his, he brought her cut finger up to eye level for inspection. Her pulse thrummed at his touch, and the soapy-clean scent that clung to him teased her nose and left her light-headed.

"Do you have some antibiotic cream or hydrogen peroxide for this? We should clean it."

Holly snatched her hand back and flashed a nervous grin. "Um, yeah…I'll get it."

Drawing deep breaths to calm herself, Holly hurried to the laundry room to fetch her first-aid kit.

"How old are your kids?"

Captivated by the melodic quality of his deep voice, Holly didn't immediately register the question he'd asked until she returned from the back room and handed him the kit. "I'm sorry. What?"

He motioned to her refrigerator, covered with the artwork of young hands. "I asked about your kids. I saw the drawings and various other cartoon-themed stuff around the house and was wondering about your family."

"Oh, I... The kid stuff is actually mine. You know the saying, 'Growing old is mandatory, growing up is optional'? That's me. A big kid." When he quirked an eyebrow and an amused grin, her cheeks heated, and she returned a sheepish smile. "But I think my active inner child helps me relate better to my students. The drawings are from my class. I teach kindergarten at Pine Grove Elementary." She paused, a stab of regret pricking her heart before adding, "I don't have any kids of my own."

"I'm sorry. I didn't mean to bring up a touchy subject." His soft tone washed over her like a balmy breeze. "I just assumed—" He frowned as he dabbed antibiotic ointment on her cut. "But I should know better than anyone not to assume anything," he added under his breath.

She lifted a curious gaze to study the knit in his brow as he worked on her finger. "What do you mean by that? That you know better than anyone about assumptions?"

His gaze collided with hers, and she held her breath, mesmerized by the emotions that flickered across his face in rapid succession. "Just that...unsubstantiated assumptions can lead to trouble. False presumptions, my own and other people's, pretty much destroyed my old life."

A swarm of questions buzzed in Holly's brain. Perhaps, like bees, the questions were better avoided. Matt's history was his own business, not hers.

Holly's heartbeat thudded a noisy cadence in her ears as Matt deftly wrapped a plastic Scooby Doo bandage around her cut finger. "There. All done."

As he returned the first-aid items to the box and clicked the clasp in place, curiosity got the better of her. "What happened, Matt? How did you end up on the street?"

His gaze snapped up to hers, bright with emotion. For long seconds, he didn't answer. He held her stare, his breathing shallow and uneven. As if he felt trapped. Panicked. Edgy.

Had she pushed too far? Crossed a boundary she shouldn't have?

Finally she broke the spell of his steady gaze and turned away. "Forget it. It's not my bus—"

"It was more a chain of events really. Like dominoes falling, one thing led to another until I had nothing left," he murmured, the distant look in his eyes telling her that his mind was back in that place and time when his life took a nosedive. Seeing the pain that dimmed his expression, she regretted her nosiness.

"My life became a runaway train, picking up momentum as it careened toward a final crash and burn. I couldn't do anything to stop it."

A viselike ache wrenched Holly's lungs, and empathetic pain flowed through her body.

"I'm so sorry," she whispered, her voice hoarse. She reached for Matt's hand, wanting him to know she understood loss, if not the full extent of his story.

When her fingers brushed his, then squeezed, Matt's gaze darted back to hers. He pulled his hand away, slowly shaking his head. "It's my own fault. None of this would have happened if I'd realized… If I'd known—" A muscle in his jaw jerked as he clenched his teeth and sucked in a sharp breath. "It all started when my wife died…when Jill…killed herself."

Chapter 3

Holly gasped, and her eyes glittered with moisture. "Oh, Matt. You can't blame yourself for her death."

"Sure, I can. And so do plenty of other people." Matt swallowed hard, choking on the bitterness and grief that swelled in his throat.

"False presumptions..." she murmured.

Matt nodded. He fisted his hands and stepped back.

Why had he said anything? He hadn't wanted to spoil the camaraderie they'd shared this afternoon. But she'd asked the one question he'd hoped she wouldn't, and he wouldn't lie to her. Even if he didn't tell her the whole truth, the whole sordid story, he owed her an honest answer in return for her kindness.

The endearing pink flush that had stained Holly's cheeks since he'd come downstairs from his shower now drained from her face, leaving her complexion wan and bleak. Matt hated the sadness and turmoil that crept into her green eyes. His explanation, vague as it was, cast a pall over the friendly meal he'd hoped to share with Holly before going back to town. He'd been looking forward to sharing her company for a couple hours, free of the suspicion and guilt that still dogged him.

The strident ringing of her telephone startled them both out of the morose and awkward moment he'd allowed them to get mired in.

Holly sidled past him. "Excuse me. I should answer that."

Matt scrubbed a hand over his face and shook off the haunting memories, the sights and sounds of those dark days after he found Jill's body in his study.

With a shudder, he shifted his thoughts to Holly's invitation to dinner. *Keep it light. Keep it casual. Then get out.*

Holly answered the rotary-dial wall phone and tucked it under her ear.

"Oh, hi, Jana," Holly said, sending him an apologetic look and holding up a finger as she mouthed, "Just a minute."

He waved off her concern and strode over to the salad she'd been fixing to continue chopping vegetables.

"Thanks, but I have plans tonight. I have company for dinner, then I need to make another quick trip to town. It was an impromptu thing... No, I don't think you know him." She flicked a self-conscious glance toward him and nibbled her lip. "It's nothing like that. Don't get any ideas. No...I—"

The pink stain returned to her cheeks, and Matt acknowledged again how attractive Holly was. But as lovely as her face and physique were, what really caught Matt's attention was the sparkle in her green eyes, the glow in her cheeks, the joie de vivre that radiated from her—in spite of her tragic loss.

Her bright disposition was contagious. Being around her, Matt found it easier to be optimistic about his future, and he grew more determined to set his life back on an upward trajectory.

Holly finished her call and pressed a hand to her still-flushed cheek. "That was my husband's sister inviting me over for the evening." She curled her lips in an embarrassed grin. "I think the idea that I'd made my own plans for Halloween night shocked her. Ryan's family has been wonderful about looking out for me since his death, but they seem surprised whenever I make steps toward moving on with my life."

He acknowledged her with a smile, then dragged a hand along his jaw, hesitating. "Would it be rude of me to ask how your husband died?"

"No, it's a legitimate question." She inhaled deeply as she met his eyes. "He was murdered."

Matt's pulse tripped. He'd expected anything but that. Cancer. A car accident. Even suicide like Jill. But *murder?*

"I'm so sorry. That had to have been such a shock."

She pressed her lips in a taut line, nodding as she turned toward the counter.

"Have they caught the person responsible?" he asked, hoping he wasn't pushing a touchy subject.

Holly lifted the lid from the Crock-Pot to stir the chili, then paused and shook her head. "No."

Sympathy speared his chest along with pain, honed razor-sharp by his own losses. "I haven't given up hope that his murderer will be caught one day, but I'm slowly coming to terms with the fact that we may never know what really happened. The best the police can figure is he was killed by a mugger who stole his shoes, his wallet and his watch."

Matt's gut tightened.

Where did you get that watch?

Flipping his wrist, he extended his arm. "A watch like this one, I take it."

She glanced up from stirring their dinner, and the color drained from her sculpted cheeks. "I—well, yes."

Without hesitation, he unfastened the clasp and turned the timepiece over, offering it to Holly. "My wife inscribed mine. You can look if you want."

She frowned and shook her head. "No, I…I believe you. You don't have to prove anything to me."

He sighed and squeezed his wife's gift in his fist. "I just wanted to alleviate any doubt you had."

Holly bit her bottom lip and, after a brief hesitation, took the watch from him. "To Matt with all my love, Jill," she read aloud. She turned the watch over and stared at it with moisture puddling in her eyes. "It's lovely. I know how much you must treasure it."

He nodded as she handed the timepiece back. "It's very important to me."

Primarily as a reminder to him of how he'd failed Jill.

How he'd neglected her because of his work. How he'd taken her for granted. How he'd let her slip into a deep depression without him noticing.

Pushing down the drumbeat of guilt, he rebuckled the strap and inhaled the peppery tomato scent of their dinner. "Dinner smells delicious. What can I do?"

She hitched her head toward the cabinets. "Spoons are in that drawer, by the refrigerator. Everything else is ready, I think. I'll serve."

Matt let his gaze roam as he fetched spoons to the table. The airy yellow curtains and cheerful floral wallpaper matched his impressions of Holly. The Big Bird clock and Snoopy cookie jar added a touch of whimsy that left him curious to learn more about the active inner child Holly boasted about. The collection of drawings taped to the refrigerator touched a raw spot inside him, reminding him how much he missed his own children. Not having his children around as they grew up was the hardest thing to accept about his current situation.

But he *would* change his circumstances, reclaim his children and get his life back on track. Or die trying.

"So you're a teacher." Matt paused between bites of chili and salad and gave her an encouraging smile. "Tell me about your class."

Holly set her spoon down and pressed a hand to the jittery

flutter in her stomach. Their get-to-know-each-other chitchat and her fascination with his ruggedly handsome face and brilliant blue eyes made this dinner feel more like a first date than just the good deed she'd intended.

Sure, she could have packed his chili in a disposable container for him to take when she drove him back to town. And she admitted his good looks factored into her decision to serve dinner as a sit-down affair, but—

Heat unrelated to her spicy chili crept up Holly's neck when other connotations of the word *affair* waltzed through her mind. She imagined Matt's startling blue eyes hazed with lust and his full lips drawing close to hers for a kiss....

Holly erased the picture with a quick shake of her head. Clearing her throat, she focused on his question. "I love my class. They're angels. All fifteen of them." When he raised his eyebrows skeptically, she amended, "Well, most of them are angels. I do have a couple who are more of a handful. But seeing those eager faces every morning, being around all that childlike innocence and energy keeps me going on days when I'm dragging." She smiled and took another bite of salad. "I wouldn't trade my job for anything. Sometimes it feels like I'm getting paid to play all day. I mean, where else could I read stories and color pictures and sing songs and play games, all cleverly disguised to reinforce writing the alphabet and counting and learning to read?" She stabbed a tomato and aimed it at him. "Plus snacks and recess."

He chuckled, a low, rich sound that tripped pleasantly along her spine. "Sounds like heaven for that inner child of yours."

"And the mother hen. I can't wait to have my own kids, but for now, I'll settle for mothering the fifteen chickadees in my class."

"I remember my daughter's first day of kindergarten." The bittersweet wistfulness of Matt's expression melted Holly's heart. "She was so excited to be going to school. Of course, she's smart as a whip and could already read and write."

"You have a daughter?" Holly thought of the children at the Community Aid Center. Frustration ballooned in her chest that she couldn't fix the problems of every family the center served, that children slept in cars or went to bed without supper.

Matt gave her a sad smile. "I have a daughter and a son, Palmer and Miles. Seven and five, respectively."

"Where…are they?"

He wiped his mouth on a napkin and dropped it in his emptied bowl. "With Jill's parents just up the road in Iona Falls. Because of my circumstances…they're better off with their grandparents. For now." He paused, clamped his lips in a tight scowl. "I haven't seen my kids in two years."

A rock settled in her stomach. "Two years? That's horrible! Won't they allow you visitation at least?"

"No. There were a lot of hard feelings after Jill died. But…honestly, I don't want Palmer and Miles to see me like this."

"But, Matt, you're their father! They need you in their life regardless of—" She caught herself, unsure how to finish the sentence.

He lifted his eyes to hers, his steely gaze a testament to his determination. "I intend to get them back. As soon as I can. But…I need a better place to live than the run-down apartment where I am now." He grunted his dissatisfaction. "The Woodgate doesn't even have working showers in the community bathroom. I can't subject my kids to those conditions. And I need to find another job."

Holly seized the opening to do a bit of prying, looking for a way to help Matt. "What kind of job are you looking for?"

He shrugged and gave her an awkward grin. "Anything that pays. I can't afford to be as picky now as I might have been in my younger days. My kids are counting on me."

She nodded and rubbed her thumb along her spoon handle as she thought. "Do you have any particular skills or training?"

He held her gaze for a moment, seemed ready to say something but finally sighed and glanced away. "I worked with a construction crew this spring and summer. But the contractor laid off several of us a couple weeks ago when his schedule slowed down."

Holly sat taller in her chair, her heart hammering. "You've done construction? Are you good with renovation work? Drywall, molding, plumbing, that sort of thing?"

He flipped up his palm and blinked. "I suppose. I'm not an expert, but I hold my own."

Holly bit her bottom lip, calculating, weighing her options, sizing up the uncertainties. An excited flutter stirred in her belly.

She could help Matt. He could help her. The plan was perfect.

"Come work for me."

Matt's eyebrows drew together in a skeptical frown. "You?"

"I'm renovating the house, and the process has dragged on far too long already. I want to be done by the end of the year, but my brother-in-law—Jon, not Robert—is doing most of the work and, frankly, he's been unreliable at best, only showing up half the time and working far too slowly. A pitfall of having a family member doing the job—hard to fire them. But...you could help him," she said without taking a breath, her hands motioning as she talked. "What with teaching, I only have weekends to give to the project right now and...well, what do you think? I'm redoing the master bathroom at the moment and still need to take out a wall in the study and fix the molding and paint and...well, there's no shortage of work. I'll make the arrangements with Jon."

Matt stared at her, looking a bit pole-axed. "I, uh...I appreciate the offer but...are you sure you want me—?"

"Why not you? You need work, and I need a reliable handyman to finish what's been started. When my husband and I started these renovations, we had no idea how much work was really needed and how long it would all take." She was chattering again, gushing without taking a breath, but she couldn't seem to curb her nervous habit. "The work was fun at first. We spent weekends and vacations hammering and painting and papering, but after Ryan died—" She curled her fingers into her hands, waiting out the stab of pain that assailed her.

"The project lost its meaning," Matt finished for her. "The fun was gone, but the work was still unfinished."

Her breath caught, and she gaped at him. He'd nailed it. But how did he know how she felt, where her thoughts were headed?

He lost his wife. He knows. He understands.

Holly nodded. "Yes. Exactly. I just want to be done with it. It's become more of a burden now than a hobby. Jon, Ryan's brother, took the job on as a favor to me, but he has other responsibilities. He's a firefighter for the county department down in Crenshaw, and he works one day out of three, has a girlfriend in Asheville." Holly paused for a breath, gauging Matt's expression. Mostly he looked shell-shocked.

She had a way of doing that to people—overwhelming them with her chattering, her openness. Her blind trust in the goodness of people worried her family, but her gut instincts had never let her down. Even Ryan, Mr. Methodical Thinker, had learned to trust her sixth sense about people and impromptu plans.

"Will you help me? I'll pay you what I would pay a contractor. I'll talk to Jon about it and make all the arrangements."

Matt opened and closed his mouth, speechless for the moment. "I…don't have a car or any way to get out here every day."

"Oh." She gnawed her lip some more as she thought. "Well, I'll come get you on the weekends and drive you back to town when we're done for the day. And I could pick you up around three o'clock when I leave the school, so you could get about four hours of work done in the evening. I'll fix us dinner, then take you home."

He still looked dubious. "That's a lot of driving back and

forth over the mountain for you. Are you sure about this? Why would you do this when you don't even know me?"

Holly rocked back in her seat, rattled. "I thought it was a good solution to both our problems. I…I've already had Robert vet you. You don't have a record. You could give me the name of the guy you worked for this summer for reference, and…I plan to check you out through the Community Aid Center records. But…" She smiled. "I'm guessing I won't find anything worrisome. You seem like a good guy to me."

He returned a lopsided grin. "I try." Lifting a shoulder and giving his head a befuddled shake, he offered her his hand. "All right. Pending your reference check and consult with Jon, I accept. With gratitude. I will finish your renovations for you."

"Great." Holly's grin rose from somewhere deep inside her and blossomed on her lips. This plan felt right. "You can start tomorrow."

After dinner, Holly gave Matt a quick tour of the house, showing him what she'd already accomplished and what needed to be done. Based on the state of the unfinished rooms, Holly and her late husband had been ambitious and visionary in tackling the old farmhouse. But the transformation was amazing. Holly had breathed new life into the old house and made it a warm home.

Matt followed Holly up the curving staircase, admiring the polished wood railing and beautifully sculpted posts. He found himself caught up in Holly's enthusiasm for the project and the allure of transforming the house, restoring it to its previous glory.

The guest bathroom where he'd showered had new brass fixtures and white tile but no wallpaper, and the carpeting in the halls was threadbare and ratty. Clearly floor coverings were a final step, once the other work and painting were finished.

"In here." Holly flipped on the light in the master bedroom, and his attention gravitated to the king-size bed that monopolized most of the floor space. The covers were unmade and rumpled as if she'd just tumbled out after a restless night. A light floral aroma hung in the air and teased his senses. He could too easily imagine Holly's lithe body tangled in those sheets, and his thoughts strayed to the hidden pulse points where she'd dabbed her flower-scented perfume.

A hot throb of desire coalesced low in his belly, and his body tightened. Gritting his teeth, Matt diverted his gaze, fighting the surge of his libido. No matter how attractive he found Holly, no matter how long it had been since he'd been with a woman, he had to keep his physical interest in his new employer firmly under control. Holly had placed a mountain of trust in him by hiring him, and he wouldn't do anything to betray that trust.

He appraised the rest of the room in a glance. Judging from the plush blue carpet and ornate crown molding, the renovations of the bedroom was complete.

"We did this room and the kitchen first, since we use them most," Holly said, confirming his suspicion. "But plumbing intimidated Ryan, and we put off doing the master bathroom. And put it off. And put it off." She turned on the bathroom light and stepped back for him to enter. "But its time has come. I'm ready to tackle the bathroom, whatever it takes."

Matt surveyed the stained linoleum floors and ancient fixtures. Outdated wallpaper peeled from the walls and hung limply over the cracked mirror. He had his work cut out for him. But he could do the job. His duties with the crew this summer had included plumbing work and basic tiling.

No problem.

But he'd get a how-to book from the library, just in case.

"So that's about it." Holly jammed her hands in the back pockets of jeans that fit her like a second skin. "By my estimates, we can be done by mid-December, Christmas at the latest, barring any snafus."

Matt winced and held up a finger. "Hey, don't even mention snafus. You'll jinx us."

Chuckling, Holly hit the light switch and backed through the bathroom door. "Don't tell me you're superstitious."

"Let's just say I've had enough bad breaks to know better than to tempt fate."

"Touché," she tossed over her shoulder as she glided toward the bedroom door.

Matt fell in step behind her, then hesitated when a picture on her nightstand caught his eye. A wedding portrait.

Pricked by curiosity, he eased closer to her bed and bent to get a closer look at Holly, wearing the same dress she'd donned as a costume for the party today. Her sculpted face had been captured skillfully by the photographer's lens. Her hair and makeup perfect, she positively glowed. But what truly made Holly beautiful was the love in her eyes as she beamed at her husband.

Matt gave the man a cursory glance.

And froze.

Recognition tickled his spine, and icy fingers of shock and dread squeezed his chest. Matt's limbs felt leaden. His blood roared in his ears.

If he could point to one person who had caused him the most trouble, the most anguish, the most loss in his life, he'd have to point to the man in Holly's wedding picture.

Had Holly told him her last name? Should he have figured it out before now?

Matt shook his head, struggling for oxygen. Fighting back the bitter taste of bile that rose in his throat.

He'd told Holly he'd help her with renovations. They'd shaken on it, and Matt wouldn't go back on his word. He wouldn't break the trust she'd placed in him.

Even if Holly's late husband had ruined Matt's reputation and destroyed his life. Ryan Cole was the ruthless ADA who'd disputed Matt's sworn statement that Jill's death was suicide and prosecuted him for murder.

Chapter 4

"Jeepers, my arms are killing me!" That Saturday, Holly rolled her tired shoulders and shook the ache from her arms. After almost two hours of reaching above her head, scraping the stubborn old wallpaper off her bathroom walls, her muscles throbbed. She glanced across the small room, where Matt tackled the hard-to-reach parts of the wall behind the claw-foot tub. "This is taking way longer than it should. What did they use to glue this paper up, anyway? Some revolutionary super epoxy?"

He grinned up at her from his awkward position on the floor. "My dad used to say, 'You can do it quickly, or you can do it right.' Quality work takes time."

"Your dad must have known my husband. Ryan was a perfectionist."

When she mentioned her husband, Matt stilled, his mouth tightening slightly before he forced a grin and turned back to the wallpaper in the corner. She'd noticed a similar reaction earlier in the day and mentally bit her tongue. She probably talked about Ryan too much, especially considering Matt had lost his wife not too long ago. Perhaps the reminder of her late spouse stirred painful memories for Matt of his loss. She'd have to be more careful about raising touchy subjects.

After stretching the muscles in her hand, she picked up her scraper and attacked the dingy, stuck-on wallpaper again.

"Tell me about your family," Matt said, breaking the awkward silence a moment later. "You said earlier you moved to Morgan Hollow when you married Ryan. Where is your home?"

"Well, I consider Morgan Hollow home now. But my family is in Lagniappe, Louisiana. That's where I grew up."

Matt propped on one elbow to glance up at her and wrinkled his nose. "*Lan...yap?* That's kind of a funny name for a town."

She laughed. "*Lagniappe* is a Cajun French word that means *something extra*. It's a great place to live, to raise a family, to grow old."

Matt turned up a palm. "So why haven't you moved back?"

She drew a deep, thoughtful breath. "I've considered it. But...it felt like a step backward somehow. Like admitting defeat after Ryan died." Her gaze darted to Matt's when she realized how quickly she'd broken her silent pledge not to keep bringing up Ryan. But Matt stared at a spot on the side of the bathtub, his gaze distant, so she continued, "Besides, I love this old house—pain-in-the-butt that the renovations are—and I have a job here I love, so..."

Her gaze connected with his, and the brilliant blue shade of his eyes stole her breath. How could she forget from one moment to the next how stunningly bright and piercing his eyes were? A tingle raced through her blood, and she let her gaze drift to the angular cut of his jaw, dusted again with dark stubble, and the definition of his muscled arms. Matt Rankin positively exuded masculinity, and the confines of her tiny bathroom only made Holly more aware of the man in her presence.

"Don't you miss your family?" he asked, his voice pitched low. She shook herself from the thrall of his sexy lure and focused on his question as she returned to scraping. "Sure. I'm especially close to my sisters, but we talk on the phone all the time. I go back to Lagniappe for special occasions. My older sister, Paige, just got engaged, so there'll be bridal showers and her wedding coming up…plenty of reasons to head back to Louisiana for a long weekend here or there."

"And your parents?"

"Dad is the founder and CEO of Bancroft Industries, a medical research company. He plans to retire in the next couple of years, and he's been grooming Paige's fiancé, Brent, as his replacement. He and Mom have been married for forty years, and they're just as much in love today as they were when they got married." She paused and rubbed her aching shoulder. "As much as I love my folks, they can be a little bit overprotective. It was actually kind of nice to move to North Carolina when I married Ryan. As a newlywed, I needed a little breathing space. My parents mean well, but they would've tried to run my life and Ryan's for us."

"Your family sounds great. You're lucky to have their support." He paused, and a sadness drifted over his face that arrowed to her heart. "Don't ever take that for granted."

She acknowledged his admonition with a slow nod. Ryan's death had taught her that lesson well. "So how about you? Are you from Morgan Hollow?"

He hesitated then grunted, "Naw."

"Then where are you from? How'd you end up here?" When he didn't respond, she glanced over at him. "Matt?"

He scooted out from behind the tub and sat up, leaning against the wall with his legs bent, his arms propped casually on his knees. He stared hard at the scraper in his hand, furrowing his brow as if contemplating a troubling topic.

She shifted her weight awkwardly, uneasy with the silence. What had she said that had darkened his mood? "If you'd rather not discuss—"

"I'm originally from Charlotte. That's where I practiced for ten years…until my wife—"

When he paused again, Holly waited patiently for him to continue, giving the wallpaper removal a half effort. She made a mental note of the term *practiced* regarding his career but was loath to interrupt him for an explanation now.

"After Jill died, I…moved to Iona Falls, because I wanted to be closer to my kids, even if my in-laws wouldn't let me see them. Then I found a job working construction here in Morgan Hollow a few months later, so I moved again. I guess I was looking for a fresh start in a new town where no one knew—" He stopped abruptly and darted a sharp glance at her. His Adam's apple bobbed as he swallowed, then he rolled one palm up. "Where no one knew about Jill's death, where I could start rebuilding my life."

The grief in his eyes stabbed Holly, stole her breath for a moment. She knew exactly the pain that had motivated his longing for a change of scenery. "Dozens of times in the past few months, I've wanted to flee my life and start over somewhere people don't know me. I'd go somewhere people don't look at me with pitying looks in the grocery store and avoid using Ryan's name as if it were taboo. Somewhere people don't pat my hand as they size me up like they expect me to have an emotional breakdown any moment." She shook her head and huffed a humorless laugh. "Moving on is hard when the people around you won't let you put the past behind you."

"Tell me about it." Matt gave her a peculiar, measuring scrutiny. "You said your husband's killer hasn't been found?"

Biting the inside of her cheek, she shook her head.

His gaze burrowed into hers, insightful, warm, understanding. "That must make it harder to move forward. The unanswered questions would drive me crazy." His tone was gentle, a balm to her ragged emotions.

Holly squared her shoulders. "The unknowns bug me, yes. But I intend to get answers. Somehow, someday. Ryan deserves justice. But I try not to dwell on the questions anymore, not at the expense of living for the present, planning for the future."

A gentle grin touched his lips, and he nodded. "Good for you."

A thump sounded downstairs, followed by a male voice calling, "Holly? You home?"

"Upstairs!" she shouted back.

Matt sent her a curious look. "Were you expecting company?"

"That's Jon, my brother-in-law who's helping me with the renovations. I gave him a key so he could work even if I wasn't home." She set her scraper down and gauged their progress with an encompassing glance around the bathroom. "How about a break? I'll make a pot of spiced cider, and we can eat leftover sugar cookies from my class's Halloween party."

Matt rose to his feet and rubbed the muscles at the back of his neck. "You're not paying me to sit around and eat cookies."

"Hey, I'm the boss." She sent him a mock scowl. "And I say it's break time. Besides, I want you to meet Jon. You'll be working with him a lot in the coming weeks."

"Holly?" Jon called again from the hall.

"Coming." She headed out to meet her brother-in-law, signaling Matt to follow her. She stepped out into the hall just as Jon reached the top of the stairs. Jon, a fireman in a nearby town, had the thick chest and wide shoulders of a man who kept his body in top condition for his job. Like Ryan, he had the Cole family's brown hair, straight narrow nose and dark eyes.

Her brother-in-law's smile of greeting dimmed as his gaze shifted to Matt. A puzzled frown dimpled Jon's forehead for a moment before he schooled his face. "Hey, I thought I'd work on sanding the floor in the study today," he said by way of greeting. "But if you're...entertaining—" He cast another meaningful glance toward Matt.

Holly supposed having a man in her bedroom on a Saturday morning could look suspicious...if she were the sort to bring men home for one-night stands. Which she wasn't. And Jon knew that. She gritted her teeth and sent him a scowl, primarily for the awkwardness his comment might have caused Matt.

"Jon, this is Matt Rankin. I've hired him to help with the renovations."

Her brother-in-law arched a dark eyebrow, reflecting his surprise, but he quickly molded his countenance in a polite smile, offering his hand to Matt, as Holly completed the introduction.

"We've been removing the old wallpaper in the master bathroom." Why she felt compelled to explain why Matt had emerged from her bedroom she wasn't sure. If she wanted to *entertain* men in her home, she could—without having to answer to Ryan's family.

Jon narrowed a scrutinizing gaze on Matt and scratched his chin. "Have we met before? You look awfully familiar."

Matt's casual stance stiffened slightly. Not much, but enough for Holly to wonder about his reaction to Jon's question.

"Not…that I'm aware of."

Jon continued to study Matt's face intently. "I know I know you from somewhere. Do you go to Mac's gym? Calvary Baptist Church? Work for a first-response squad somewhere locally?"

Matt shook his head, his expression wary. "No. None of the above. Sorry."

"Oh, well, maybe it will come to me later." Jon shrugged and turned his attention back to Holly. Pitching his voice low, he stepper closer to her. "I told you I'd help you finish the house. You didn't have to hire anyone. Extra help is an unnecessary expense when I'll work for free."

Holly cut a side glance toward Matt, who feigned interest in the family photos on the wall, before facing Jon again. "And I appreciate your help more than you know. But you're busy with Kim and working at the fire station, and I'm ready to be done with this old house. I want to finish by Christmas if possible."

Both of his eyebrows shot up now. "By Christmas? It'll take more than one guy working round the clock to finish in two months."

Holly grinned and patted Jon's arm. "Which is why I still need you to come when you can and pitch in, if you're willing."

"Of course, but—" He left the complaint hanging, glancing once more to Matt before sighing his resignation. "Whatever. It's your house."

"Yes, it is. So…we were just about to take a break. Would you like some spiced cider?" Holly started down the stairs but tossed the question over her shoulder.

"Uh, no, thanks," Jon answered, his gaze fixed on Matt again. "I thought I'd get started sanding the floor in the study today. You still want to keep the hardwood floor in there, right? Sand the existing floor, then stain and finish it?"

"Yep. That's the plan."

The soft thud of footsteps on the stairs told her Matt was following her as she made her way to the kitchen. She moved her Snoopy cookie jar from the counter to the table and removed the lid. "Help yourself. The mother of one of my students made them."

Matt pulled out a kitchen chair with a scrape and sat down. He ate one of the cookies in two bites and closed his eyes as he savored the treat. "Mmm, can't tell you the last time I had a homemade cookie. These are delicious."

"I'll be sure to tell Mrs. Holbrook you enjoyed them." Taking a seat across from him, she nibbled a cookie herself, and her mind drifted back to something Matt had said earlier. "What did you mean when you said you *practiced* in Charlotte before you moved to Iona Falls? What did you *practice?*"

Matt seemed startled by her question. He drew a deep breath and blew it out, then rubbed his bristly chin before answering. "Medicine."

"You're a doctor?" Holly blinked her surprise.

Again, he hesitated. "A pediatrician."

Holly thought back with fresh understanding to Matt's quick actions at the community center when the little boy choked on his candy. "But you don't practice anymore?"

He shook his head, a dark regret shadowing his eyes.

"Why not?"

Matt shifted in his chair, and he met her gaze with a decidedly uncomfortable look.

She realized how pushy and personal the question was and backpedaled. "Never mind. It's none of my business."

"No, it's a legitimate question. But the answer is rather long and complicated." Frowning, Matt glanced away for a moment before returning a penetrating gaze to Holly. "I want you to know the truth. I want to be honest with you." He scraped his palm across his jawline and groaned. His face reflected a deep, gnawing misery. "But I'd rather save this discussion for another day."

"Of course." Curiosity plucked at her, but she shoved it down. If Matt didn't want to talk about his reasons for giving up medicine, she had no right to push him. Clearly his past was a painful topic. Could his resignation from medicine be related to the death of his wife?

A resounding ache gripped her chest when she considered all he'd lost. Not just his wife and custody of his children, but his career, his livelihood as well. What tragic secret was Matt harboring? Had she been wrong to bring him into her home without knowing more about his past?

Cold fingers of foreboding wrapped around her heart. Robert had said Matt showed no criminal record, but his arrest history only told part of the story.

"I was thinking about that stained glass you recovered."

Matt's comment pulled her from her troubling thoughts. "What about it?"

"Well, as heavy as it is, it's going to take two men to install it. We should probably make arrangements with Jon to do that project next time he's here."

Holly nodded her agreement. "I'll ask him about it."

"You still want to cut a place for it over the front door?"

"Yeah, I think so. That seems like the best place to me. What do you think?"

"I think you're the boss, and it's your decision."

She scowled at him. "You're no help."

He chuckled, and the rich, low rumble from his throat sent a sweet frisson of heat shimmying through her. "Okay, you want to know what I think?"

She angled her head and lifted her eyebrows, inviting him to continue.

"I think that stained glass is more than just a beautiful piece of art. I think it's a reflection of who you are and where you are in your life."

Holly was ready to ask him what he meant, the words were on her lips, when he reached for her hand and closed his warm fingers around hers. Her heartbeat stuttered, and her gaze flew up to meet the rich warmth of his. "You've been through a lot of pain because of the death of your husband. But you're soldiering on. You're surviving. And like the bird in that window, you're testing your wings again and taking flight. I think that stained glass deserves a prominent place in this house as a testament to the way you're rebuilding your life."

"What choice did I really have? My only other option was to lie down and die, to wallow in my self-pity. What kind of life is that?"

A shadow passed over his face. "No kind of life at all." He squeezed her hand tighter, and a bright intensity flared in his eyes. "I know, because that was the choice I made, and I suffered the consequences. I have no one to blame but myself for the shape my life is in now, but I'm determined to turn it around, to get back on my feet…and eventually get back to medicine."

She smiled her encouragement, then sent him a teasing scowl. "Not before I finish my renovations, I hope. A deal is a deal."

Matt's face lit with amusement. "Don't worry. I keep my promises. I'm yours for as long as you need me."

Holly's breath faltered. She'd had similar promises from her family and Ryan's. She'd never been truly alone after Ryan's death, but Matt's pledge to stick by her filled her with the sense of well-being she hadn't known in a long time. The sense that she and Matt were kindred spirits flowed through her again. She knew somehow that he needed the friendship and support she offered him as much as she needed the warmth and understanding he offered. By leaning on each other, they were both stronger.

He still held her right hand, and she stacked her left one on top of his. Holding his gaze as firmly as she gripped his hand, she whispered, "And I'm here for you, too. Whenever you're ready to talk, whenever you need anything to get back on your feet. I believe in you, Matt. Your life's not over. I predict many wonderful, happier times in your future."

His muscles tightened beneath her touch, and surprise flickered in his expression before morphing into heartbreaking longing and gratitude. Too soon, he sucked in a sharp breath and tore his gaze away. Clearing his throat, he withdrew his hands from hers and shoved his chair back from the table. A stark emptiness washed over her as soon as he pulled away.

"I'd better get back to work. My boss has a tight deadline for finishing her renovations, and I don't want to get fired for lollygagging on the job." Despite his teasing comment, his voice sounded thick, tense, and she puzzled over the shift in his mood.

"Don't you want your cider? It will only take a moment for me to heat it in the microwave."

He shook his head and silently disappeared up the steps to the second floor.

For a moment, she sat alone at the table, wondering if she'd said something wrong, something that offended him in some way. She was certain there'd been a connection between them, that, before he'd withdrawn, she'd seen the same sentiments that filled her heart reflected in his eyes. But something held him back. He still had protective walls erected. Her heart twisted with sympathy and longing. She wanted so deeply to reach past those walls and know the real Matt. Her instincts about him told her he had so much to offer, a deep well of love and compassion.

Give him time.

After putting the cookie jar away, she headed back upstairs, following the low drone of male voices. She found the men in the study, where Jon was readying the floor sander.

Matt was moving furniture to the hall, out of their way, and gave Holly only a quick glance when she entered the room. "If it's all the same to you, I think I'll leave the wallpaper stripping for another day. Jon could use my help sanding and staining this floor."

Holly shrugged. "Sure. Whatever. It all has to be done sometime."

She left the men to work, but disappointment pricked her as she returned to the master bathroom. She'd enjoyed the camaraderie she'd had this morning as she'd worked with Matt. His company had made stripping wallpaper a less tedious task.

By late afternoon, Holly had given up on scraping her bathroom walls, and Jon and Matt had finished sanding the study floor. Holly propped her shoulder on the door frame, watching the men clean up their supplies.

"Well, Holly, I'm calling it a day. Kim and I made plans for tonight, and I better get home and get cleaned up." Jon wiped his hands on an old rag, then tossed it aside. "Matt, I appreciate the help. I guess I'll see you next weekend, and we'll tackle the first coat of stain."

Matt unplugged the sander and began coiling the electric cord. "Actually, I can handle the staining this week. I'll apply a coat Monday night when I come over and add the second coat a couple days later once the first one's dried."

Holly didn't miss the irritation that flickered across Jon's face. She'd always assumed her renovations were more of an inconvenience, a family obligation to Jon. But his reaction to

Matt's help made her think he was a bit more territorial about the project.

Matt shucked off his work gloves. "Holly's got a piece of stained glass she wants mounted over her front door. That's gonna be a two-person job. Maybe we can do that next weekend?"

Jon's jaw tightened, and he arched an eyebrow before shooting Holly a curious look. "What stained glass? You never mentioned stained glass to me before."

"It's a window I salvaged from an old church in town."

Jon's expression grew suspicious. "A church? You don't mean *the* church, where…"

He left his sentence hanging, but Holly knew where his thoughts had gone. "Yes."

Jon stared at her, saying nothing, clearly battling his emotions, shock, disapproval and revived grief straining his composure. She knew he still felt the loss of his brother deeply, even if he tried not to show the extent of his grief.

When Jon picked up his toolbox and brushed past her, she caught his arm, stopping him. "You know, I really appreciate all you're doing for me."

He shrugged and kept walking. Holly followed him to his truck, undaunted by his sullenness. "I didn't hire Matt because I doubted you. He needed a job, and I was eager to be through with this mess. It was a win-win situation. If his presence bothers you—"

"Holly, it's your house, your decision who works on it." Jon stowed his tools and slammed the storage box on the back of his truck closed. "My only concern is for your safety. I don't like the idea of you being alone out here with him. How well did you check this guy out before you hired him?"

"I had Robert run a background check on him. He has no record, and he's been nothing but a gentleman with me. I trust him."

Jon furrowed his brow and glanced back at the house. "I just can't shake the feeling that I know him. And not necessarily in a good way. I've got a bad feeling about him, Holly. It's nothing I can put my finger on, but my gut is telling me that he's trouble."

Chapter 5

Holly lifted her chin. "My gut disagrees. I like Matt. I trust him."

Jon frowned his disapproval but gave her shoulder a quick squeeze before yanking open the door of his truck. "I hope you're right. Be careful, Holly. Call if you need anything."

She stepped back as he cranked his engine and drove off. Waving away the plume of exhaust and dust kicked up by his tires, she headed back up the steps to her front porch, then noticed the stray mother cat dart into the barn. The cat had settled into her new home in the barn quickly and was filling out thanks to her new diet of Cat Chow. She was still leery of her hostess, but Holly was making progress earning the cat's trust.

Holly crept quietly into the cool, dim barn and found the mother cat feeding her kittens. "Hey, pretty girl, how are those babies doing?"

The cat gave her a wary look, then returned her attention to her kittens.

"There you are," Matt said, joining her in the barn a few moments later. "So how are our furry friends doing?"

"See for yourself." Holly waved a hand toward the nest of kittens. "Their eyes are fully open now, and they're getting mobile." She glanced over her shoulder to Matt and smiled. "I think I'm going to name the mother Magic. She's so sneaky and quick. She can be here one second, and she's gone the next."

"Magic, huh? I like that." He hitched his head toward the truck parked out front. "Speaking of going, I'm ready to leave whenever you are."

Holly pulled her keys from her pocket and dangled them on the tip of her finger. "Ready."

Matt settled his hand at the base of her back as they headed out to the truck, and his proprietary gesture sent a fuzzy warmth up her spine. He opened the driver-side door for her and gave her hand up as she climbed inside.

I've got a bad feeling about him.

Holly shivered, then dismissed Jon's concerns as overprotectiveness. Matt's old-fashioned chivalry, a welcome and increasingly rare trait in the men she knew, only bolstered her confidence that she had nothing to fear from Matt.

The peak autumn colors had passed by late October, but she savored the last glimpses of red and gold in the leaves as she pointed her truck toward town. All too soon, the foliage would be gone, and the mountainous landscape would be blanketed in ice and snow.

Fatigue settled deep in Holly's bones after a long day of battling stuck-on wallpaper, and with a tired sigh, she leaned her head back against the seat.

Matt cast a side glance at her. "I could find another way to get back to town in the future. You shouldn't be stuck with driving me after a long day of work."

She shrugged and flashed him a grin. "I don't mind. It's worth it to me to get the remodeling work done."

The narrow, winding road that crossed the ridge of mountains between her farmhouse and town was as scenic as it was treacherous. What passed for a shoulder was nothing more than a small strip of gravel before the mountain dropped off steeply on one side of the road and rose in a sheer rock cliff on the other side. Tight blind curves meant she couldn't see oncoming traffic until the last second. But the Smoky Mountains held a magical beauty every season that she loved. The steep forested hills, clear mountain streams and vivid foliage were such a dramatic contrast to the flat bayou country around her Louisiana hometown.

When Holly pulled in at the low-rent complex where Matt was living, she studied the dilapidated building and the weeds sprouting from cracks in the parking lot. He'd confessed earlier in the week that the "apartment" he rented here didn't have a private bathroom, and the community bath had no hot water and a broken shower fixture. She'd been appalled at what his landlord got away with and had given him blanket permission to use the guest bathroom shower whenever he wanted.

He'd accepted gratefully, but she'd seen the chink it had put in his pride to have to ask. Matt deserved better, and her heart ached, wishing she could do more.

Matt rubbed the back of his neck and twisted his lips in a frown. "I know it's not much, but the rent is low, and I have a roof over my head when the temperature drops at night."

She angled toward him on the seat, embarrassed that something on her face may have given him the impression she was passing judgment. "You don't have to defend anything to me."

He shrugged. "Maybe I'm still defending it to myself. This place is a far cry from the house I had in Charlotte."

"Maybe dissatisfaction with your living conditions is the motivation you need to keep you on track to changing your life."

He tugged a lopsided grin. "I had that motivation long before I moved in this dump. Seeing Palmer and Miles again, having the means to win back custody of my family is all the motivation I need. I just let a bad case of guilt and self-pity mire me for the past couple years."

"Are you at least able to talk to your kids, to call them?"

"I call whenever I get access to a long-distance connection, but my in-laws intercept my calls."

Holly frowned. "Can they do that? Don't you have rights as their father?"

Black shadows filled Matt's face. "Jill's parents gained sole custody. I'm at their mercy."

She gaped at him. "How could the court allow that? And what grandparents could be cruel enough to deny their grandchildren access to their only living parent?"

He slanted her a rueful smile. "I appreciate your indignation on my behalf. I haven't had anyone in my corner regarding my kids in a long time."

Sitting straighter in the driver's seat, Holly lifted her chin. "You can use my phone to call your kids any time you want."

Matt's gaze softened. "Thank you, Holly."

She laid a hand on his arm and narrowed a determined gaze on him. "In fact, I think you should start now petitioning your in-laws for a chance to see your kids at Thanksgiving."

He scoffed. "Fat chance of that happening."

"You never know until you try."

He shifted a pained gaze to the crumbled parking lot. "I've been trying for almost a year to convince them to let me see my kids. The only contact they want from me is the monthly child support payments I send."

She tipped her head, startled. "Child support? How are you able to send child support?"

He waved a hand toward the run-down apartments. "It's been harder the past couple months since I lost the construction job. But I manage to scrape up a little cash each month, partly by living in this dump rather than anything nicer. I go without so that my kids don't have to."

Aghast, Holly furrowed her brow. "While I admire your dedication to providing for your children, don't you think you're taking it to an extreme? Martyring yourself and virtually living on the street can't be what your children would want for you. Have you ever thought that the money you're sending your in-laws might be better spent rebuilding your life, providing yourself the means to reclaim the life you lost?"

Matt's jaw grew rigid and his eyes darkened. "My comfort means nothing compared to my kids'. I'd rather starve than think for a minute that my children didn't have every advantage possible."

"Don't your in-laws have the means to care for them?"

"That's not the point. How can I justify using money on myself that—"

"—could help assuage some of your guilt over not being there for them?"

He shot her a sharp glance, and her heart kicked. She'd crossed the line. What right did she have to question Matt's choices?

Her cheeks heated. "Sorry, I shouldn't have said that."

Matt dragged a hand over his face, frustration and regret lining the corners of his eyes and mouth. "But you're right. Maybe if you'd been around to kick me in the pants a year ago, I wouldn't have wasted so much time before getting my head on straight. But with everything that happened after Jill died, I—" He shook his head and sighed. "Well, there's a lot of history between me and my in-laws. A lot of pain, a lot of misunderstanding."

"Are you saying they're depriving you of your children out of spite?" Disbelief and outrage tightened her voice.

Matt's only answer was a poignant half smile, before he popped open the passenger-side door and slid out of the truck. "Thanks for the ride. What time do you want to get started tomorrow?"

Holly flopped back against the driver's seat, her mind spinning and the injustice of Matt's situation roiling inside her. She took a deep breath to clear her head. "I—I'm supposed to go to church and then lunch with Ryan's sister and her husband. They live here in town, so…I should be able to pick you up by about two o'clock."

Matt jerked a nod. "Works for me." He held her gaze for a long time, a myriad of emotions swirling in the depths of his dark eyes. "Holly, I— You don't—" He exhaled harshly and shook his head. Finally he pressed his lips in a tight line and stepped back. "Be careful driving home."

Disappointment plucked at her that he hadn't been able to tell her what so clearly weighed on his heart. She hoped that in the coming days he'd trust her more, open up to her about the events that had sent his life spiraling down the tragic path it had taken.

Holly watched as Matt ambled across the parking lot. His loose-limbed stride and the confident set of his shoulders gave no indication of the deep pain he harbored. As she pulled back onto the road and headed home, she racked her brain for some further means to help him. The first step was to break through Matt's defenses, to earn his trust.

"Matt, I need your opinion." Holly crossed the study floor and squatted beside him.

"Okay." He abandoned the strip of quarter round he'd been replacing and sat back on his heels. "I think college football should institute a play-off system."

Holly chuckled. "Well, I agree, but that doesn't answer my question." She held up three small samples of wallpaper. "Which one of these do you like best for the master bathroom?"

Matt shoved to his feet and took the samples from her. "Do you want me to be honest?"

She lifted an eyebrow. "It is the best policy."

Shifting his weight, he suppressed the niggling guilt that he hadn't yet told her about his history with her husband and focused on the scraps of paper. "Then my answer is none of these. I think you should paint." He handed the samples back to her.

She scoffed. "Paint? Paint is boring."

"But it's also easy. The truth is I've never hung wallpaper before, and it kind of intimidates me."

She flicked a hand, waving off his concern. "It's really not as scary as it sounds. You'll be fine."

He shrugged. "You're the boss."

"And you haven't answered my question." She thrust the three samples toward him again. "Which one?" Before he could answer, Holly's doorbell pealed. "Hold that thought. I'll be right back."

When Holly answered the door, Jana's husband, Robert, waited on her front porch. She appraised his police uniform and flashed a teasing grin. "I didn't do it, officer. I was framed."

He leveled his shoulders and gave her a mock scowl. "That's not what the evidence says, ma'am."

Grinning, she stood back to let him in. "To what do I owe this pleasure?"

His shrug fell short of casual. "Just checking in to see how you are, how the renovations are going."

Holly folded her arms over her chest and narrowed a dubious look on him. "Curious. You've never been interested in my renovations before."

"So maybe I was in the neighborhood."

"More likely, you talked to Jon, and you're here to check out my handyman."

Robert feigned surprise. "You hired a handyman?"

"Don't pretend you didn't know." She angled her head and arched an eyebrow. "So what did Jon say?"

"Only that he was concerned with the situation and wanted me to look into it."

Holly scoffed and rolled her eyes. "Does the term *overprotective* mean anything to you?"

Robert hitched up his gun belt and gave her a smug grin. "Protect and serve, that's my job."

The thud of a hammer reverberated from the second floor, and Robert cut his gaze to the stairs. "He's here?"

Holly sighed. "Yes, and I'll introduce you if you promise not to act like you're here to interrogate him. Be friendly and pretend that you're interested in the renovations. I know that's a stretch for you, but…"

Before she could finish, Robert was halfway up the stairs. She followed and showed him to the study, where she made introductions.

Matt eyed Robert's uniform warily but offered a smile and his hand. The men shook hands, and Holly pointed out the wallpaper samples.

"You're just in time to help me pick out a pattern for the master bathroom."

Robert shook his head. "Oh, no, you don't. You're not gonna suck me into this. If it were up to me, I'd have just slapped some paint on the walls months ago and been done with it."

Holly twisted her mouth in frustration. "You're no help."

"I just call them as I see them."

When Robert locked a predatory look on Matt, Holly rallied. She wasn't about to let Robert grill Matt like some common criminal. She took her brother-in-law by the arm and dragged him toward the door. "I'm sorry you can't stay longer. Next time bring Jana, and we'll have lunch, okay?"

At the top of the stairs, Robert pulled his arm from her grip. "Subtle."

"You got what you came for. You met Matt," she whispered.

Robert glanced back toward the study before descending the stairs. "What do you know about this guy? Where did you find him?"

"I know that he needed work and that he has construction experience. That's all most people know when they hire a handyman. Am I right?"

"Maybe so, but—" Robert's gaze narrowed on the stained-glass window which had been propped against the wall in the foyer since they'd unloaded it three days earlier. "What's this?"

"Isn't it pretty? I salvaged it from that old church they tore down in town."

Robert shot her a disgruntled frown. "That church was condemned for a reason, Holly. Going inside was dangerous and foolish."

Holly stiffened at his superior tone and pressed her lips in a firm line. She met Robert's challenging glare with her own. "Maybe so, but…I went in because I felt closer to Ryan there. I wanted to see where he died once more before the place was demolished. The police haven't given me many answers about his death, so I was looking for clues of my own."

"And did you find any?"

Robert's cool tone rubbed her the wrong way, but she shoved down her irritation in deference to her relationship to Ryan's family. "Maybe I did." She nodded to the stained glass. "This was in the room where Ryan died."

"I thought it looked familiar. I remember seeing it the night Ryan—" Robert stopped abruptly and cut an apologetic look to her.

"You saw the stained glass the night you found Ryan?"

Robert gave a tight nod. "He asked me to meet him at the church to help him with something. Could have been to save that window."

But by the time Robert had arrived, Ryan was already dead.

Holly faced the window, staring at it as if it held the answers to Ryan's murder. "I know he'd have loved it. He'd have wanted it just like I did when I saw it. I just wish I knew…"

Where did she start? There were so many unanswered questions.

Bracing his hands on his hips, Robert sucked in a deep breath and let it out in a whoosh. "I'm sorry, Holly. The unknowns frustrate me, too." He raised a dark gaze and aimed a finger at her. "But that's no excuse for you to have gone into that condemned church. Leave the investigation to the police. I promise you, we're doing everything we can to bring Ryan's killer in. Finish the house. Plan a trip. Go see your family. The best thing you can do now is put his death behind you and move on with your life."

A sharp pain sliced through her, and Holly wrapped her arms around her middle in a vain effort to staunch the ache. "I'm trying."

He touched her shoulder gently, then slipped out the door without further comment.

Holly stood in the foyer, staring at the stained glass long after Robert left. The hollowness that always filled her when she discussed Ryan's death returned but didn't seem as overwhelming today. Maybe time *was* healing her wounds.

Like the bird in that window, you're testing your wings again and taking flight.

Matt's assessment stirred a warmth in her blood that chased out the gloomy chill of grief. Squaring her shoulders, she resolved to install the window before completing any other renovation projects. Not only did the window serve as a beautiful reminder of Ryan, but the hope and renewal depicted in the image of the dove buoyed her spirits.

And she'd need all the inspiration she could get to make it through the holidays alone.

Or would she be alone?

She glanced toward the stairs. Matt didn't have anyone this holiday, either. Perhaps they would survive the loneliness of the coming weeks by spending it together.

The prospect of sharing Thanksgiving and Christmas with Matt brought a smile to her lips. Maybe a special holiday season, filled with all the joy and promise of Christmas, was just what Matt needed to start healing the pain from his past.

Holly intended to find out.

In the days that followed, Matt immersed himself in the remodeling and repair projects at Holly's farmhouse. He stained the floor in the study, helped Jon install the stained glass over her front door and began tearing out the old plumbing in the master bathroom. Having something productive to do and seeing the tangible results of his efforts filled him with a sense of purpose and accomplishment that gave his spirits a healthy boost. Sharing time with Holly, though, was a mixed blessing.

As much as he treasured their growing friendship, he struggled with the knowledge that he was keeping vital information from her. Through his silence about Ryan's part in his past, he was living a lie, a deception based on omission.

But once he completed the renovations for Holly, he would move on, and she didn't have to ever know who he really was.

Just do the work and get out of her life. No harm, no foul.

He could almost convince himself he had nothing to feel bad about. Then Holly would bestow another piece of her trust in him—giving him a key to the farmhouse, loaning him her truck to make a trip to the hardware store—and the nagging guilt would gnaw at him again.

His uneasiness over keeping his past from Holly became more tangled when he acknowledged his attraction to her. More than an awareness of Holly's beauty, the pull Matt fought was organic, rooted deep inside him. His senses crackled on high alert when she was near. Thoughts of her filled every waking hour and taunted him in his sleep. She fascinated him, tempted him, challenged him, encouraged him. She made him feel more alive than he had in years.

One November afternoon as he raked leaves in her yard, she strolled toward him from the house, carrying two glasses of lemonade. Leaning on his rake, he paused to appreciate her gracefulness, the shimmer of sunlight in her hair and the pink tint the cool autumn afternoon painted on her cheeks. As always, his body thrummed, and she captivated his attention.

She handed him one of the glasses, then motioned to the pile of leaves behind him. "Raking my yard isn't your job."

He shrugged. "I don't mind. After spending most of the day

around varnish fumes, I thought the fresh air would do me good. Besides, it won't be long before the weather turns cold."

"True. Well, suit yourself." Holly sipped her drink, and Matt caught a glimpse of purple on her chin.

A bruise?

He stepped closer for a better look. "You have a mark on your throat, under your chin."

She raised a hand to her neck. "Where?"

When he guided her hand to the spot, he felt the hitch in her pulse under his finger. "It looks like—"

"Paint. We had art today in class. I always come home with paint in the strangest places."

He quirked an eyebrow as bittersweet memories assailed him. "I can remember Palmer coming home from kindergarten with glitter in her hair or paint on her shoes. Art days were always interesting."

Her answering grin washed through him like a balmy breeze. Holly's smiles always involved her whole face—bright eyes, glowing cheeks and a flash of teeth.

Then she tipped her head, her expression turning speculative. Matt chuckled. "What's that look for?"

She set her glass on the ground and took the rake from him. "I was wondering if you wanted to go with me to the Community Aid Center tomorrow. I'm supposed to be volunteering there and thought you might like a day off from renovations."

Matt stuck his thumbs in his pockets. "I don't need a break. I enjoy the work and staying busy. And if we're going to get done by Christmas, days off are a luxury I'm not sure we can afford."

She collected the leaves he'd raked into a taller, neater pile then propped the rake against the nearby maple tree. "I'm not cooking dinner tomorrow. I always eat at the center on the nights I volunteer…if that influences your decision." She flashed him an impish grin.

Matt folded his arms over his chest and admired the spark

of sunlight that danced in her eyes. "So if I want to eat tomorrow, I should listen to the boss and tag along, huh?"

"Something like that." She turned her back to the leaves and toppled backward. The pile scattered as she flopped into it and tossed handfuls into the air with childlike glee.

He sent her a playful scowl. "Do you know how long it took to rake those up?" He waved a hand toward her, grinning. "Look what you did to my pile."

Wiggling her eyebrow, she scooped an armful of fallen foliage and hurled them at Matt.

"Hey!" he said in mock affront as he bent to toss a large handful on her in return.

Holly's peals of laughter tripped through him, warming his heart. As a battle of flying leaves erupted, his spirits lifted. Cutting loose, acting silly and enjoying Holly's playfulness felt good.

When, at last, he collapsed beside her in the scattered remains of the leaf pile, his laughter joining hers, he sighed contentedly. "I used to play like this with Palmer and Miles. Their favorite game was to have me bury them in leaves so they could burst out and scatter the pile everywhere like a Tasmanian devil." When she laced her fingers with his, he gave her a bittersweet smile. "I miss the simple moments like that with my kids the most."

Holly squeezed his fingers and brought his knuckles up for a light kiss before releasing his hand. "You'll have more moments like that with them."

His body jangled from the warm brush of her lips, and as he fought down the surge of fire in his blood, he frowned. "I don't know that."

Scowling at him, Holly narrowed a fierce gaze. "I do. And you have to believe it, too, if you want to make it happen."

"I have to be realistic, Holly. I may never—"

"No." She sat up and met his eyes with fire and conviction filling her face. "*Can't* never could. That's what I tell my class.

The first step to achieving something is believing it can happen. Don't stop believing, Matt. You will get your children back. I know you will."

Matt's heart swelled, full to bursting with the faith she gave him, the hope she inspired. "You're amazing. You know that? I don't think I've ever met anyone with your optimism and can-do strength."

She seemed startled by his assessment, leaning back and cocking her head at a curious angle. "Well...thanks. I try. It's easier to be all sunshine and roses when you're talking about someone else's life instead of your own. I've had my share of defeatist moments since Ryan died. Especially when I consider the fact that his killer has never been caught."

She chewed her bottom lip and idly tore bits from one of the maple leaves.

"They'll catch his murderer." He stilled her fidgeting hands with his own, and her gaze darted up to his. Matt's pulse throbbed, and he longed to pull her into his arms and kiss away the doubts that dimmed her eyes. "Believe it, Holly."

She tugged up one corner of her mouth. "Follow my own advice, eh?"

He tweaked her chin. "That's about the size of it."

After pushing to his feet, he offered her a hand up, trying not to think about how perfectly her hand fit his or how right touching her felt. Leaving at the end of her renovation project would be hard enough without harboring any notions of what he'd be losing when he said goodbye to her.

Chapter 6

The next day after school, when Holly picked Matt up, they drove to the Community Aid Center as planned. She headed into the kitchen, where the other volunteers had already started the evening meal, and was surprised when Matt followed her. When she gave him a quizzical look, he took an apron off one of the hooks by the door.

"I came to serve, not be served," he said simply before finding a place at the counter where the meal was being prepared and rolling up his sleeves.

Holly nudged her way in beside him, layering sliced ham on the bread he spread with mustard before passing the sandwich to the next volunteer for lettuce and tomato. The assembly line produced fifty sandwiches in record time, and Holly and Matt moved on to heating soup and putting cookies on a tray.

When the dinner line opened, Holly ladled vegetable soup while Matt passed out bags of potato chips to those who wanted one.

During a lull in the dinnertime traffic, Holly glanced at Matt and found him staring at the crowded dining room with a heartbreaking expression on his face. "What is it, Matt?"

He snapped his gaze to hers as if jolted out of his thoughts and shook his head. "It's just not right for so many children to be living out of cars or sleeping in alleys. What kind of life is that for a kid?"

"A hard one," she agreed softly, touched as much by his concern as by her own worry for the homeless families.

A mother with two young girls approached them and helped her daughters fill a tray with food. While she helped one daughter pick a cookie for dessert, the older girl began coughing. Matt focused on the older child whose deep, croupy coughing continued for nearly a minute.

Without a word, Matt left the serving line and circled through the kitchen out to the floor of the dining room to intercept the mother and her daughters.

Holly held her breath, watching as Matt spoke to the mother, then knelt in front of the sick child. He laid a hand on her forehead, frowned, then pressed his ear to her chest. The girl took several deep breaths for him before another bout of coughing seized her.

Deep lines creased Matt's brow, and as he rose to his feet again, he guided the mother to a corner away from the crowd.

Concerned, Holly left her spot in the serving line, as well, and joined Matt and the mother in the far corner.

The woman was shaking her head as Holly approached. "I don't have money for a doctor, and even if I did, I couldn't afford the medicine." The woman lifted a shoulder, though her expression didn't match the indifference of the shrug. "She's had colds before, and they always go away in time on their own."

"She doesn't have a cold. She has pneumonia, and if she doesn't get an antibiotic soon, she might need to be put in the hospital." Matt's grim expression told Holly just how critical the child's condition was. A muscle in his jaw tensed as he shifted his attention back to the little girl. "If I gave you a prescription, is there any way you could fill it tonight?"

The mother rubbed her thumb on the palm of her other hand, gnawing her bottom lip until it bled. "I told you. I don't have money for medicine."

Matt's jaw tightened again, the muscles jumping. "Do you not have Medicaid or some other financial assistance? It's very important. Left untreated, pneumonia can kill a child her age."

Tears filled the woman's eyes, and Holly had seen enough. "I'll pay for the medicine."

Both the mother and Matt turned startled looks toward her as she stepped forward. Holly took the mother's hand in hers and met her disbelieving stare.

"I'll go with you to the pharmacy and pay for a full course of whatever antibiotic Matt thinks is best. We're going to get your baby girl well. I promise."

"But—"

"No buts." She hitched her head toward the door and smiled. "Let's go now before Hill's pharmacy closes."

Tears dripped from the woman's eyes. "Oh, ma'am, how can I ever thank you?"

Holly patted her hand. "You just did."

"That was a wonderfully generous thing you did tonight," Matt said as she drove him back to the low-rent apartment where he lived.

She dismissed his praise with a shrug. "It was nothing. What's a few dollars compared to saving a child's life?" In the dim cab of her truck, the dashboard lights played across the rugged cut of his jaw. Even in the low light, compassion and kindness shone from his eyes. "You're the one who was alert to the girl's need, caught her illness so it could be treated before she became critical."

"I've heard that croupy cough enough times to recognize it

instantly. I'm just glad I came with you today and that I made the effort to keep my medical license up-to-date so I could write her script. Where would that girl be if we hadn't helped her?"

Holly nodded, stared at the road spotlighted by her high beams and squeezed the steering wheel. "I'm afraid her case isn't unique. We get sick kids through the center all the time. It's heartbreaking."

When she heard Matt huff in disgust, she cast a side glance at him. His face was rigid, tense with emotion.

"What?"

He shook his head. "There has to be something we can do, some way to get those kids the help they need."

Holly's chest filled with a sweet warmth. Matt, who had so little of his own, who faced the monumental task of regaining custody of his children, who scrimped to find the money to get back on his feet, was passionately concerned over the well-being of the homeless children in their community. If she'd had any doubts about her choice to employ Matt, to allow him into her life, they vanished.

Along with another piece of her heart.

Matt grew dearer and more important to her every day. His thoughtfulness, his compassion, his sinfully handsome smile nestled deep in her soul.

"Maybe we can do something," she offered. "Where there's a will and all that…. Perhaps between us, we can figure something out?"

He stared out the windshield a little while before glancing her way. "Food for thought, huh?" He laid a hand on her arm and gave her a gentle squeeze. "Thanks for the ride. See you tomorrow?"

She nodded. "Right after school."

As he disappeared inside the dilapidated building he called home, an idea took root in her mind. By the time she reached her farmhouse, she'd examined her plan from every angle. She'd worked through every drawback, justified every argument and enumerated all the benefits. Just the same, she wanted someone to bounce her idea off of, someone to tell her that she wasn't crazy.

Still sitting in her truck, she picked up her cell phone and began dial.ng her older sister. She knew practical, cautious Paige would help her make a reasoned and rational decision.

But logic and prudence weren't what she wanted. She needed someone to share her enthusiasm and excitement, someone to tell her it was okay to follow the tug of her heart. So she dialed Zoey's number instead.

"Hey, sis, how's Siberia?"

Holly chuckled. "Why don't you come visit me and find out?"

"Tempting, but…I met somebody—his name's Derek, and he's so hot!" Zoey's enthusiasm crackled over the phone. "Anyway, I was thinking I'd spend Thanksgiving with him. Are you horribly disappointed?"

A pang settled in her chest. She saw so little of her sisters since she moved to North Carolina, every missed holiday hurt. "Well, sure, I'll miss seeing you, but that's not why I called."

"Oh? What's up?"

"I want to ask Matt to move in with me."

At the other end of the connection, Zoey made choking noises. "You're going to what?"

"Not in some romantic way," she amended. "But it makes sense for practical reasons. I've rationalized all of the pros and cons—"

Zoey groaned. "Now you sound like Paige."

"Well, I don't want to be rash. But this feels right, and…I wanted your opinion." Holly elaborated on her plan to help Matt, and as predicted, Zoey loved the idea, applauded Holly's willingness to take a risk and demanded a detailed account of Holly's past several weeks with Matt.

"Are you sure that practicality is all that's behind this idea? I mean…do you have feelings for him? Do you think this thing with him could become serious?"

Holly's heart pattered. "No, it's nothing like that. We're just friends. Besides, I don't think he's in a place in his life right now to even consider a relationship."

"Too bad. He sounds great. What about down the road, once he gets his ducks in a row?"

Holly grinned. Since shortly after Ryan's death, Zoey, who seemed to have another new boyfriend every time they talked, had been pushing her sister to get back into a relationship.

"Well, we have a great rapport. In fact, sometimes I feel like he can read my mind. Having lost his wife, I think he understands how I feel, even before I do. It's obvious he's well-educated, and we can talk about almost any subject. He's got a wonderful sense of humor, and I...have fun with him—if you can call stripping wallpaper and ripping out old plumbing fun."

"I wouldn't call anything that you're doing to that house fun." Zoey paused. "Look, I gotta run. Derek just got here, and we're going to see that new Tom Hanks movie."

"Okay, have fun."

Zoey laughed. "Don't I always? Hol, I say go for it with Matt. But you really don't need my approval or anyone else's. If it feels right in your heart, do it. You've always been a good judge of people. Listen to your instincts. 'Kay?"

"Thanks, Zoey. Love you."

Holly snapped her phone closed and shut her eyes, picturing Matt's warm smile. A sweet contentment filled her chest.

Listen to your instincts.

Her mind made up, Holly entered her vast, lonely farmhouse eager to lay out her idea for Matt.

Tomorrow, she would invite him to move into one of her spare bedrooms, to live with her at the farmhouse while he helped with the renovations.

"Living here will not only give you more time to work on the renovations, but it will also save me all those trips back and forth across the mountain. I'll save on gas and time, and you can move out of your current apartment and save the money you were spending on rent."

Matt opened his mouth to object to Holly's proposal, but she chattered on, her enthusiasm glowing in her eyes. He hadn't been in her truck five minutes that Friday afternoon, three weeks after he'd started working for her, before she'd begun laying out her idea and detailed reasoning.

"And the sooner you build up your savings, the sooner you can get on your feet and the sooner you can file a motion to win back custody of your children." She barely paused for a breath. "It's a win-win situation. I'll get my house finished that much sooner, because you can be there all day while I'm at school, and you'll be one step closer to having your kids."

How could he argue with anything that would bring him closer to his kids?

Matt rubbed the five-o'clock shadow on his chin, debating her tempting offer. The idea of living under the same roof with Holly filled him with a complicated mix of trepidation and temptation. Fighting his attraction to her was difficult enough without adding the intimacy of cohabitation, and he needed only to remind himself who her husband had been to know why pursuing a relationship with her was a bad idea.

His plan was to finish the renovations on her house and slip quietly out of her life. She need never know the role Ryan had played in ruining his life. Keeping the full truth from her rankled, but Matt didn't want to jeopardize the chance she'd given him. He needed the renovation job, needed the salary she was paying him. But more important, he needed this time with Holly. She filled him with hope and optimism. The time he'd spent getting to know her these past weeks had been among the happiest days of his life.

How would she feel about him if she knew her husband had prosecuted him for murder? Holly's faith in him had gone a long way toward restoring his belief in himself. He wasn't sure he could stand to see even a shadow of doubt or disillusionment in her eyes should she ever learn of his sin of omission.

"So what do you say?" Holly's expectant gaze found his, and her eager smile nudged aside the doubts that whispered warnings in his ear.

"All right. I accept." He inhaled deeply, praying he'd made the right choice. "Thank you."

They stopped at the hardware store on the way to her farmhouse and bought a few supplies for the next project on her list—refinishing the staircase banister and stairs. As they were leaving, they ran into her brother-in-law Jon in the parking lot.

"I was just about to buy some more PVC pipes to finish installing the new sink in your master bathroom tomorrow," Jon told Holly. "If you want to hold up a bit, I can load it in the back of your truck to take home now."

"No need," she replied. "Matt replaced both the sink and the toilet earlier this week."

Jon raised his eyebrows and squared his shoulders. "Is that so?"

Holly nodded. "But we ordered a new shower stall unit. It's on back order now, but when it comes in, I'm sure Matt will need a hand with that."

Jon's gaze shifted to Matt. "Just let me know. I'll be glad to help."

Matt detected a note of sarcasm in Jon's tone, undoubtedly due to a feeling of being supplanted on the renovations at Holly's house. The last thing Matt wanted was to cause friction in her family.

"So what's all this?" Jon motioned to the bags in their hands.

"We're working on the banister and stairs this weekend." Holly flashed her brother-in-law a smile that indicated she hadn't picked up on the underlying tension in Jon's voice. "Feel free to join us. It should be a blast."

Jon removed his Red Sox baseball cap and scratched his

head. "Hmm, refinishing stairs or bowling with the guys from the fire department? Tough one."

Holly snorted. "You don't bowl."

Jon tugged his mouth into a lopsided grin and nudged Holly's chin with his fist. "Which is why you can count on me to be there first thing in the morning." He divided a glance between Matt and Holly. "Listen, why don't I pick you up in the morning on my way out to the farmhouse? Save Holly a trip into town."

Matt rubbed his chin. "Thanks, but…"

When he hesitated, Holly jumped in. "He'll already be at the house. I've invited him to take one of the guest rooms."

Clearly the news shocked and disturbed Jon. His brow furrowed in a deep V, and grabbing her arm, he dragged Holly aside.

Matt bristled protectively and stepped forward, only backing off when Holly raised a hand and signaled for a moment alone.

He loaded their purchases on the backseat of Holly's truck, giving Holly the illusion of privacy for her discussion with Jon. But he shamelessly perked his ears to listen to the exchange, monitoring them from the corner of his eye. Although Jon was her brother-in-law, Matt experienced a primal urge to protect and defend Holly. He followed their tense exchange with all of his senses on full alert. If he got even an inkling that Holly needed him, he wouldn't hesitate to come to her defense.

As Holly finished her discussion with Jon, Matt met the other man's hard glare squarely.

"Ready?" When she got into the truck and cranked the engine, he climbed in beside her.

"Is there a problem? If my moving to the farm—"

"There's no problem, Matt. What I do with my life is none of his business. I think it's just hard for them to see me moving on. I think they feel I've forgotten about Ryan. I assured him that wasn't the case and that I had given this decision careful consideration." She backed out of her parking place and waved to Jon as they pulled away.

Matt held Jon's stare as they drove out of the lot. "Still...he doesn't look happy. I don't want to be the source of trouble for you with Ryan's family."

Holly dismissed the comment with a wave of her hand. "He'll get over it. He just doesn't want to see me get hurt."

Matt clenched his teeth, guilt kicking him in the gut. He didn't want Holly to get hurt either, but he knew the longer he withheld the facts about who he really was, the deeper his secret would cut when she learned the truth.

Chapter 7

Between special holiday activities at school and the ongoing renovations at her house, the days before Thanksgiving flew by for Holly. Having Matt sharing her roof gave her lonely farmhouse more energy, more life than it had had in months. And, by turn, his presence complicated things more than she'd expected.

Emotions that she'd kept in check when she only saw Matt a few hours each day ran rampant with her new housemate around. Sharing meals and a bathroom with him—since the master bathroom was still in upheaval—added a familial intimacy to their relationship Holly hadn't considered when she had examined her plan.

Brushing against him as they passed in the hall or catching his eye over her morning oatmeal caused goose bumps on her arms. Hearing him hum in the shower or bumping hands as they washed the dinner dishes together stirred a fluttering in her veins. The magnetic pull she felt toward him strengthened daily.

One day at school, she'd just finished passing finger paints out to her class when her thoughts drifted to Matt's comment about his daughter coming home from kindergarten sprinkled with glitter. No doubt, Matt had been a terrific father, before…

She remembered how comforting and compassionate he'd been with the girl at the Community Aid Center. Pediatric medicine was a good fit for him. And he seemed the perfect fit for her. He—

"Ms. Cole, Tommy won't share the green!"

Snapped out of her romantic notions by her student's complaint, she shoved thoughts of a relationship aside. Matt might be charming, intelligent and devastatingly handsome, but he had no interest now for anything more than friendship. His single-minded focus on reclaiming his life, his good name and his children made that point clear. Though he touched her often, the contact was always brief and platonic—a squeezed shoulder as a greeting in the morning, a sympathetic hand on hers when she shared a concern, a casual stroke of his palm on her cheek when he said good-night. Yet every pat or lingering glance stoked the longing that smoldered inside her.

Every time her romanticism reared its head, Holly doggedly tamped down her growing attraction to Matt, knowing her feelings for him would make him uncomfortable and their living arrangement awkward. She knew, also, that Matt would go out of his way not to hurt her feelings, but that inevitably she'd end up with a broken heart if she didn't nip her growing feelings in the bud.

Matt didn't want or need the complication of a romantic entanglement. The protective wall he kept between them, his silence regarding his past spoke for the distance that remained between them, despite the facade of intimacy created by shared chores and cozy breakfasts.

Thanksgiving morning dawned sunny and cold. After bundling into her thick terry bathrobe, Holly traipsed down to the kitchen where the scent of freshly brewed coffee and cinnamon rolls teased her senses.

"I could get used to this." She poured herself a mug of coffee and flashed a groggy smile to Matt. Sighing contentedly, she took a long sip of the hot brew. "Waking to the scent of breakfast cooking is my idea of heaven."

A returned smile dimpled Matt's cheek. "I love a woman who savors the simple pleasures."

Holly studied his sleep-rumpled hair and stubble-dusted chin, and her pulse kicked. The crisp scent of soap from his shower drifted to her, and a pair of well-worn sleep pants rode low on his lean hips. Even first thing in the morning, Matt was pure masculine sensuality.

Holly's hand tightened around her cup, and determined to sidetrack the sexual path of her thoughts, she turned toward the pan of sweet rolls he'd heated. If she couldn't satisfy the lusty cravings he stirred, she could at least sate her appetite for sweets.

"After you went upstairs last night, Jana called to make sure we knew you were invited to dinner today. We're supposed to be there by noon, and she plans to eat at one. So…wanna come with?"

Matt licked cinnamon roll icing off his thumb before answering, and Holly's belly quivered imagining those lips sucking her fingers, her earlobe, her—

Stop it!

"I don't think so," he said.

She blinked. What had they been talking about?

He propped a hip against the counter and shrugged. "Thanksgiving is a family day, and I'm not family. I'd feel like I was intruding."

"Jana invited you. You're more than welcome to join us. Jon's bringing his girlfriend."

"That's different. We're not a couple. Our relationship is a business arrangement."

A knot twisted in her gut. Though she'd known how he felt,

hearing him state his opinion of where they stood so bluntly was sobering. Disappointing.

She shoved down the bubble of hurt that swelled in her chest. She'd figured they were at least friends, something more than just business acquaintances, but she nodded her understanding.

"All right. I don't want you to feel out of place." She finished her coffee in a few gulps and put a cinnamon roll on a napkin to take upstairs. "Well, if I'm going to get my casserole and pie made before it's time to go, I'd better hit the shower."

By the time she finished dressing and made it back down to the kitchen to cook, Matt had disappeared to the study, and the pungent scent of polyurethane wood stain told her that he was at work.

Once she had her food prepared and loaded in her truck, she checked in with Matt once more before she left. "I'm going. Are you sure you won't come along?"

He lifted his stain-smudged hands and flashed a melancholy grin. "No, thanks. You have fun."

Holly's heart stumbled. Matt was right. Thanksgiving was a family day, and he had to be missing his kids today more than usual. How could she leave him here alone?

"I won't stay late," she promised. "We'll have leftover turkey and pie together tonight, okay?"

He winked at her and returned his attention to the crown molding he was staining.

Thoughts of Matt, by himself at her house and alone with his grief, plagued Holly as she drove the twisty mountain road into town. As she parked in her in-law's driveway, she swore to herself she'd find a good excuse to leave Jana and Robert's early.

Robert met Holly at the front door with a highball glass in one hand, which he raised in greeting. "Happy Thanksgiving. Can I get you a drink?"

"A little early to be drinking, isn't it?"

He shrugged and took another sip from his glass. "It's Thanksgiving, and I'm celebrating. I have lots to be thankful for this year."

She acknowledged him with a smile. "Thanks, but I think I'll pass until dinner's ready." She held out the casserole. "Speaking of which, I brought sweet potatoes, and there's a pecan pie on the front seat. Will you get it?"

"Sure." Robert set his drink down on an antique washstand in the foyer and headed out to her Tacoma.

As Holly carried the casserole into the kitchen, she inhaled the tempting scents of sage dressing and roasting turkey. Jana, a petite, female version of her brother Ryan, turned from the stove with a bright smile. "I thought I heard new voices. Is Matt with you?"

"No, he stayed home. I think he felt like he'd be a fifth wheel."

"Nonsense." Jana took the casserole from Holly and slid it into the oven to warm. "The food will be ready in about a half hour. Jon, Kim and Robert are watching football in the living room, if you want to join them."

"Yeah, in a minute. I—" Holly chewed her bottom lip and glanced toward the front door where she'd left Robert. "I noticed Robert's already drinking."

Jana paused in her meal preparations and glanced at Holly with a knit in her brow. "Yeah."

"I don't mean to sound like a prude but… Well, Ryan mentioned to me shortly before he died that he was worried about how much Robert drank. I'd thought it had gotten better in recent months, so I didn't say anything."

Jana rubbed the back of her neck. "Some days are better than others, but…there's nothing to worry about. If he had a real problem, I'd be the first to send him to get help."

Holly unbuttoned her jacket, debating whether she should press the issue, but opted not to. She took off her coat and hung it in the front closet on her way into the adjoining room. The professional football game on TV held little appeal to her, but she chatted amiably with Jon's girlfriend until Jana called to them that dinner was ready. Holly and Kim helped Jana carry all the food in from the kitchen, while Robert poured wine for everyone.

Holly glanced at the empty seat beside her as they all took their places at the table. While she understood Matt's reservations about joining them, she wished she hadn't had to come alone.

As usual, Jana's cooking was delicious, and they all stuffed themselves. They were eating Holly's pecan pie when Jon leaned across the table toward her. "Is Rankin still at your place?"

Holly didn't like the tone or the dark look Jon gave her. She hesitated before answering. "Yes. Why?"

"Because I can't shake the feeling that I know him, so I did a little checking on him. I don't like what I found."

Irritation scraped through her. "You've been snooping on Matt? How dare you?"

Jon seemed unfazed by her pique. "Technically Robert did the checking through his resources at the police department."

She shot a scowl to the end of the table, where Robert was pouring himself another drink. "You've been investigating Matt without telling me? I can't believe this!"

Robert took a slow sip of his drink then set it aside. "Aren't you interested to know what we found?" he asked, his words beginning to slur a bit.

She was, but she refused to condone their snooping by asking. "No! If there's anything about Matt's past that he wants me to know, then he'll tell me when he's ready. I can't believe you invaded his privacy and abused your position this way!"

"He's not who he says he is."

Holly jerked her attention back to Jon when he spoke. "What?"

Jon set his fork down and sent her a concerned look. "Robert couldn't find any record of a Matt Rankin before three years ago. At least not this Matt Rankin."

"So? I already knew he didn't have a criminal record. We established that the day I met him."

"I'm not just talking about a criminal record. I mean, there's no public record of him at all before three years ago when he showed up in Morgan Hollow."

She shook her head. "Then you're not looking in the right place. He said he lived in Charlotte before he moved here. I can't believe you checked every public record in Charlotte before coming to your conclusions."

"Better than that," Robert slurred. "I checked the state's databases. Tax records, school records, welfare records, you name it. I accounted for every Matt Rankin listed." Robert aimed his glass at her, and his wine sloshed onto the tablecloth. "He ain't there."

Holly frowned, her dinner sitting like a rock in her stomach. "There must be some mistake."

"I don't make mistakes," Robert growled. "The guy's not who he says he is."

"Which raises the question, *who is he?*" Jon added.

Holly took the napkin from her lap and slapped it on the table. "I don't know if any of this is true, but it doesn't matter to me. I like Matt. I trust Matt. I don't care—"

"Are you sleeping with him?" Robert asked with a sneer.

"Robert!" Jana swatted her husband's arm and sent Holly an apologetic look.

Shoving her chair back from the table, Holly stood. "Jana, thank you for inviting me," she said in clipped tones. "The meal was delicious, but I think I'll be leaving now."

Jon caught her arm. "Holly, don't get mad. I did this for you. If *you're* not going to look out for your best interests then someone has to."

"Who appointed you my protector? I'm perfectly capable of looking after myself."

"Ryan would've wanted me to make sure you were all right."

"I'm fine! And I don't need a keeper." She yanked her arm from his grip and stormed to the door.

Jana hurried after her. "Holly, I'm so sorry. Please don't go."

Still clutching his drink, Robert caught up with them. "If I were you, I'd ask Rankin about where he came from, what he was doing five years ago. Ten years ago." He sipped his wine, then added, "And I wouldn't be hoppin' in the sack with him until I had some answers."

Fury blazed through Holly's veins, and she barely made it out the door without saying something she knew she'd regret later. She didn't want to cause a rift between her and Ryan's family. But then, she hadn't started this. Robert and Jon had.

All the way home, Jon's and Robert's allegations haunted her.

How was it possible there was no record of Matt in any of the state's databases prior to three years ago? Assuming Robert had known what to look for. Matt had said he'd been a pediatrician. Surely there was some record of his medical practice with the state medical board. A license to practice.

Perhaps to protect their assets in case of a malpractice suit, he and Jill had registered all of their property in her name. Maybe he'd set up a corporation to facilitate his taxes with a name like ABC Pediatrics.

Plenty of options were possible to explain why Robert and Jon had not found information about Matt. Holly took a deep calming breath and loosened her grip on the steering wheel. When she got home, she'd do a little searching of her own.

No. She exhaled harshly, frustrated with herself. Looking for information on Matt without his knowledge would make her as guilty as Jon and Robert. She would simply ask Matt about her brothers-in-law's findings and give him a chance to explain.

When she got home, Holly hurried upstairs to the master bathroom, where Matt was chiseling up the old bathroom tile.

"It is a holiday, you know. You're allowed to take a day off every now and then."

Matt shifted from his knees to sit on the floor and rolled his shoulders. Holly couldn't help but notice the play of muscles under his flannel work shirt. "Not if we're going to get everything done by Christmas, I can't."

Holly propped against the door frame and grinned at him. "I hope you don't think I'm paying you overtime or holiday pay."

He chuckled. "As long as I get a piece of that pecan pie, I'll be fine."

She grimaced. "I left the pie at Jana's."

Matt clapped a hand over his heart and sent her a comically crestfallen look. As he got to his feet and dusted his hands on the seat of his jeans, his brow dipped in a puzzled frown. "You're back kind of early, aren't you? Everything okay?"

"I—" Sighing, she raked the hair back from her face with her fingers. "Actually, there is something I'd like to talk to you about."

His expression grew wary. "All right. Give me a chance to clean up, and I'll meet you downstairs."

Holly headed to the kitchen, where she started a pot of coffee brewing. Pulling a pan of leftover lasagna out of the refrigerator, she fixed a plate to reheat for Matt. A few minutes later, she heard him on the staircase and met him in the family room.

Stacked in one corner were a number of large plastic storage boxes. When she gave the boxes a curious look, Matt said, "I was down in the basement earlier, looking in the tools, and I saw your Christmas decorations in a back corner. I went ahead and brought them upstairs to save you the effort."

"Thank you." His thoughtfulness touched her. Reconciling this considerate man with the portrait of deception Jon and Robert painted of him became all the more difficult for her when her insides turned warm and mushy around him.

"I'm something of a Christmas fanatic. It's my favorite time of year, and I love dressing up the house for the holidays the minute Thanksgiving is over." She straightened a bow on the wreath on top of the stack and flashed him a self-conscious grin. "I do try to keep the two holidays separate, if only by a matter of hours."

He returned a breathtaking smile. "Somehow I guessed that about you." Poking his hands in his back pockets, he faced her, his expression open. "You wanted to talk about something?"

Her gut clenched. Questioning him about his identity, about his history, in light of his continued kindness toward her seemed petty. Her heart told her that she could trust Matt, so why did she listen to Jon and Robert? Why did she let them confuse her and make her doubt her instincts?

"This is going to seem really rude and nosy…and I wouldn't ask except…" She rubbed her palms on the legs of her slacks. "It seems Jon and Robert were concerned about you living here…about them not knowing much about you. Since Ryan died, they've been a bit overprotective of me. Their hearts are in the right place, but their methods at times—"

"Holly, stop." His low, quiet tone jolted her as much as if he'd shouted. Matt's eyes were dark, his mouth pressed in a taut, somber line. "I think I know where this is going."

She crossed the floor to him in three quick steps, catching his hands in hers. "I don't want to pry into things that are none of my business, Matt. I know there are things in your past that are too painful to talk about, but…if I don't answer their questions about you, if I don't give them something to answer their suspicions, they'll only keep digging and causing trouble and—"

He cupped her jaw with his palm, stroked her cheek with his thumb. "Tell me what they said. What upset you?"

His gentle touch calmed her jitters a little, but she was still uncomfortable with putting him on the spot this way. "They…ran a search for you in the state databases, and they claim there's no record of a Matt Rankin matching your description before three years ago."

He inhaled deeply, his nostrils flaring and the muscle in his jaw twitching. "That's because before three years ago, Matt Rankin didn't exist."

Holly's heart thundered. Surely she had heard him wrong. "What are you talking about?"

"My real name isn't Matt Rankin. It's Matt Randall."

Chapter 8

His muscles taut, Matt waited for some flicker of recognition in Holly's expression, but all he saw was hurt and confusion. If his name meant anything to her, she was playing her cards close to the vest. Considering that the Holly he'd gotten to know over the past few weeks wore her emotions on her sleeve, he found it difficult to believe she was hiding her reaction now.

When she only stared at him with an incredulous expression, he delved into his explanation. "I started using the name Rankin three years ago in an attempt to put some distance between me and the ugliness that my life had become. The name Matt Randall had a stigma attached to it, and that stigma followed me wherever I went. I couldn't get a job, couldn't write a check at the grocery store without getting dirty accusing looks." He shook his head. "Not that I really cared what the people at the store thought of me. But I figured out pretty quick that for the foreseeable future, my name had been ruined."

Holly tipped her head, her eyes brightening with insight. "The false allegations you mentioned earlier…."

He sighed. "Yeah."

"What—"

He raised a hand to cut her off. "Let's sit. It's a complicated story."

With a hand under her elbow, he guided her to the couch. He settled beside her, his legs splayed and his arms propped on his thighs. Dragging a hand down his face, he struggled for the courage to tell her what he knew he must. He owed her the truth.

He just prayed she wouldn't hate him when he'd finished spilling his soul, his darkest secret to her. Matt angled his head toward her and met her worried gaze squarely. "I was accused of murder, Holly."

She gasped, and her eyes rounded in horror. "Murder? But…who? A patient?"

He shook his head. "They thought I'd killed Jill. The spouse is always the first suspect in a violent and untimely death. When Jill died, I automatically became suspect number one for the police. That's the false allegation I told you about. That's how I lost my pediatric practice, my kids, my good name."

Color drained from her face, and despite her shock, he could see that she was sorting through a flood of questions, assimilating this new information with everything he'd told her in the past, grappling with the mind-blowing ramifications that crashed down on her like a devastating meteor shower. When her hands trembled, he longed to hold them in his own and soothe the tremors that shook her.

But his comfort would be rebuffed, no doubt. Until he'd explained the whole sordid truth, his touch would be unwelcome, tainted. He grieved the loss of the small intimacy they'd shared, that tentative level of trust and affection.

Holly drew a slow deep breath, the confusion and betrayal in her gaze sliced him to the quick. "Matt…you said Jill killed herself, that it was suicide."

"It was. But there was enough circumstantial evidence the night of her death for the police to arrest me. I didn't help my case much, either. I told them her death was my fault."

Holly stiffened and fisted her hands on the edge of the sofa cushion. "Why would you say that?"

"Because I believed it. On some levels, I still do."

She shook her head. "You lost me. If Jill's death was suicide, how can you believe you killed her?"

"I didn't say I killed her. I didn't pull the trigger, but I'm responsible for the state of mind she was in that night. My inattention to her needs, to her feelings, to our marriage was the reason she felt so alone that night." The bleakness and loss he'd known that night reverberated in his voice and revived the blackness that ate at his soul. "If I'd paid more attention to my wife's despondency and been less wrapped up in my job, I could have done something to stop her. I could have gotten her help. I could have fixed our marriage. I could have shown her what she meant to me before she took her life.

"But I was too self-absorbed, too busy with my patients and too certain that the depression she'd slipped into was just a passing mood swing or a bad case of PMS. I was an insensitive jerk who left his wife alone at home most nights while I stayed late at the hospital. I neglected her needs, and when she felt she had nowhere left to turn, she took her own life." His voice cracked, and he swiped at the moisture that had crept into his eyes. He sucked in a restorative breath and exhaled through his lips. "I've spent the past five years coming to terms with my responsibility, my guilt."

Holly grabbed his arm and squeezed. "Matt, stop. You can't blame yourself."

He lifted a hand to interrupt. "Believe me, I've heard all the denials and rationalizations before, Holly. I know what they say about survivor guilt, but…this is different."

"No, it's not. Jill and only Jill is responsible for her actions." The fierce determination that laced her tone sent a wisp of warmth to the icy hollowness deep inside him. If he'd had someone on his side, bolstering him, defending him, *believing in him* all those years ago, how differently would his life have turned out?

His hands fisted, frustration and self-recrimination pumping through him. "How do I forgive myself for the fights we had, for my obliviousness to the depths of her depression? How do I forget that my inattention drove her into the arms of another man?" When Holly flinched, he nodded. "She had an affair, trying to shock me out of my daze, and afterward, she suffered a terrible guilt because of her cheating. She laid it all out in the note she left me."

Holly swallowed hard and rasped, "Jill left a note?"

Clenching his teeth, he nodded once.

As she slouched back against the sofa, Holly's gaze drifted away as she processed all that he'd dumped on her. She pressed shaky fingers to her lips and dragged in an unsteady breath. "Wouldn't a note in Jill's handwriting be enough evidence that she'd committed suicide?"

"Ordinarily, yes, but—" He hesitated, battling down the surge of fury and frustration for the foolish and rash choice he'd made in a moment of panic and turbulent emotion. "I took the note. I destroyed it before the police arrived."

She snapped a startled gaze toward him. "What? *Why?*"

"In hindsight, I wish to God I hadn't." He rubbed the ache in his jaw where tension and self-reproach knotted his muscles. "At the time I wasn't in my right mind." Revived memories kick-started the turbulent grief that had overwhelmed him that day. "I'd come home from the hospital late, and…I found Jill in our study. She was sitting behind my desk, her body slumped forward. It was dark in the room, and at first I didn't notice the wounds. But…I smelled the blood. I smelled death."

He leaned his head back and closed his eyes. The grisly images flashed behind his eyelids in a gruesome slide show of memories. "She'd taken the kids to her parents' house for a visit, and then come home alone and shot herself. She—" He swallowed hard. "I'm a doctor, so the first thing I did was try to revive her. I felt for a pulse, tried to staunch the bleeding. I moved the gun from her hand and set it aside. When it began to really sink in, that she was dead, that she was gone, I was overcome with grief and shock. Even before I found her note, I knew what she had done and why. And I lost it. I lashed out, yelling and breaking things in the study. Mad at myself, mad at her, mad at the world—and consumed with pain. With loss. With guilt. I'd let her down in the worst possible way, and she'd chosen to take her life because of it."

Anguish strangled him, gripping his chest so tightly he couldn't breathe. He dug his fingers into the soft cushion of the couch and struggled to regain enough composure to continue.

A small, cold hand touched his, jarring him from his memories. His gaze darted first to his fist, where Holly had wrapped her fingers around his, offering comfort and strength. Stunned, he lifted his eyes to meet the pain and sympathy etched in her face.

After all he'd told her about his failing Jill, about the ugliness of his past and the guilt that still tainted him, how could she feel anything for him beside disgust?

"Go on," she urged, her voice gentle and understanding.

Matt gathered his thoughts and held her gaze as he continued. "She confessed to her affair in the note and apologized for it. She talked about how lonely she'd become, how confused and how overwhelmed she felt by the depression she'd sunk into. She felt she had nowhere to turn." He grimaced and bit out an obscenity. "What kind of husband allows himself to become so distant that his wife feels she has to take her life to get his attention?"

Holly squeezed his hand harder. "Matt, don't do this. Haven't you beaten yourself up long enough? There may have been trouble in your marriage, but your wife's decision to take her life was her own. You didn't make her do it."

"I'm beginning to see that…now. But at the time, I was drowning in grief and guilt. I couldn't do anything to save her, but I made a decision that night. I wanted to protect her memory, her reputation as much as I could. I didn't want anyone to find out about her affair—especially not her parents. And I didn't want her friends and family to know she'd committed suicide. Her parents are Catholic, and to them, suicide is an unforgivable sin. I couldn't heap that burden on top of the pain of losing their daughter." His eyes held with hers, and he dropped his voice to a pained whisper. "So I burned her note."

Holly absorbed the heartache in Matt's voice like a physical blow, feeling the sting all the way to her marrow. Losing Ryan had been difficult enough without feeling any responsibility for his death. She couldn't imagine the suffering Matt had endured.

"When the police arrived, I had my wife's blood on my hands and clothes, there was broken furniture and debris cluttering the study because of my outburst, my fingerprints were on the gun, and I'd destroyed the key piece of evidence that could have exonerated me. I don't blame the police for arresting me. I'd have arrested me, too. I looked guilty as hell."

A rock settled in her gut. "And you told them you were responsible for her death."

"Apparently. It's in the transcript from my interrogation. But, honestly, I was so out of it that night, I don't remember what I said." Grief lined Matt's face, and despair darkened his eyes.

She longed for a way to soothe some fraction of his sorrow and misery. "What about an alibi?"

"I didn't have one. At least not one the police could verify. One of my patients, a little girl who'd fought leukemia for six months, had died that afternoon. She was the same age as my daughter, and it hit me really hard. I drove down by the river and spent an hour or so alone just sitting in my car." He rubbed his chin, deep in thought. "Witnesses can place me leaving the hospital at eight o'clock, and the coroner estimated the time of Jill's death was around 8:45." He shook his head sadly. "I got home just minutes too late to save her, and I had no one to corroborate my alibi."

"Dear God, Matt..." So many questions swirled in her head, Holly didn't know where to start. An overriding voice of compassion said Matt had been through enough today, reviving the memories to satisfy her probing. But one issue singled itself from the rest, begging an answer. "Did...you clear up the confusion with the police?"

He raised a bleak, shadowed gaze.

"Surely your case didn't go to trial...." But the hollow expression he wore contradicted her assertion, and her heart clenched.

"There was enough circumstantial evidence for them to hold me over for trial." Matt massaged the muscles at the back of his neck. "A week later, my in-laws sued me for custody of the kids. My patients left in droves. Nobody wants a man accused of murdering his wife around their kids. Within a couple months, my practice was operating in the red, and I had to close. On top of funeral expenses for Jill, legal bills for both the criminal charges against me and the custody battle began to pile up. Without any income, I depleted my savings pretty quick. I lost my house, and because of the media coverage and my pending felony charges, I couldn't even get a job at the corner convenience store."

Holly drew a slow breath as understanding dawned. "Was that when you started using the name Rankin?"

"It was soon after that."

"And your trial?" She held her breath, almost afraid to know the truth. "What happened?"

Matt didn't answer at first. He gave her an inscrutable look and searched her face as if puzzled by her question. Just when she thought he wasn't going to answer, he shoved to his feet and paced across the room.

"I had a good lawyer who was able to point out the numerous holes in the prosecution's case. Ultimately, the jury acquitted me. But by then, the damage had been done to my reputation, my bank accounts, my family and my morale."

The weight of Matt's losses pressed down on her, squeezing her lungs and wrenching her heart. Tears puddled in her eyes. "So…you lost *everything* in a matter of months."

He dragged a hand through his hair and exhaled sharply. "Pretty much."

A bubble of grief for Matt's losses swelled inside Holly. She rose stiffly from the couch and crossed the floor to him. More than anything, she wanted to help him reclaim the life he'd lost, win back custody of his children and reestablish his medical career. The injustice of the tragedies that he'd endured nearly suffocated her. No wonder he'd felt defeated, without hope, burdened with guilt and grief.

Holly stepped up behind Matt and wrapped her arms around him. He jolted when she touched him, shuddering and tensing his muscles, before relaxing in her embrace. Slowly he turned, nudged her chin up to study the tears that pooled in her eyes, then drew her into the circle of his arms. Holly meant to offer him comfort, yet his embrace imbued her with a sense of security and peace that burrowed to her bones. The crisp smell of soap clung to him, and she savored the fresh scent.

"I'm so sorry for what you went through," she murmured, her head nestled against his broad chest. Beneath her ear, the life-affirming thud of his heart drummed a steady cadence. "No one should have to suffer the kind of losses you have."

"No one said life was fair."

Pulling back enough to meet his eyes, she pinned him with a determined gaze. She framed his face with her hands. The stubble on his jaw lightly abraded her palms, and a tingle raced through her blood. "I want to help. I want to do anything I can to help you rebuild your life and get your children back."

Tender emotion flooded his gaze and arrowed to her core.

Then a distancing veil dropped over his countenance. His brow creased, and he shook his head. "I didn't tell you about my past because I was looking for sympathy or a handout."

Holly straightened her spine. "I know that. You were just answering my questions, and I appreciate your honesty."

His eyes narrowed, and he firmed his jaw. "I don't want charity or your pity."

"I know that, too. I wouldn't insult you by offering charity. But I can't stand here, knowing all that's happened to you, and not do something to help. I care about you, Matt. I care what happens to you."

His arms tightened around her. "I appreciate your support. Truly. But putting my life back together and getting to the place I was before everything started falling apart is something I need to do on my own, in my own way. My children are all the motivation I need." A determined fire burned in his eyes. "I will get my life and my kids back. I refuse to accept anything less."

She stroked his cheeks, then pulled his head down so that she could rest her forehead against his. The warmth of his breath caressed her face. "I just want you to know that I'm here for you, for whatever you need in the weeks ahead."

"You have no idea what it means to me to hear you say that," Matt said, his voice pitched to a low, intimate whisper.

His lips were scant inches from hers. She focused her attention on his mouth as he spoke, and her heart fluttered with anticipation.

"I care about you, too. More than I should."

She tipped her head. "How can you care too much about someone?"

"You can let your feelings cloud your judgment." He slid a crooked finger along her cheek, and a shiver raced through her. "The last thing I want is to hurt you."

Holly frowned. "Hurt me? How?"

"Just by our association. If some aspect of my past ever

came back to haunt me, I couldn't live with myself if I let it taint your life."

Leaning back to better gauge his expression, she shook her head and laughed softly. "Don't be silly. How could the bygones from your past harm me?"

Matt's eyes grew stormy, and he tensed his mouth. For a moment, he only stared at her with his troubled gaze. "I pray to God it doesn't."

His evasiveness, the dark concern that etched worry lines beside his mouth left her with more questions than answers, but she didn't press him. That he'd confided as much as he had today spoke volumes for the trust he placed in her. If there was more on his mind, she hoped he'd open up to her about it eventually.

Matt folded her into his arms again, pulling her closer. His fingers combed through her hair, and he pressed a soft kiss to her head. "I'm sorry I didn't tell you any of this sooner. I wasn't trying to hide anything from you, but I wasn't sure how you'd react. I wanted more time for you to get to know me, to know who I really am, before I shared all the ugliness with you."

Holly curled her fingers into the soft fabric of his shirt and held him close. "You have nothing to apologize for. Your past is your business. You have a right to keep it private. I only asked because my brothers-in-law—"

He tipped her chin up with his thumbs. "In their place, I would've done the same thing. I know they were just trying to protect you."

She twisted her lips in a wry smile and slid her hands to the small of his back. "Well, you're far more forgiving of their intrusiveness than I would be in your situation."

The corner of his mouth lifted, but the smile didn't reach his eyes. Sucking in a deep breath, he levered away from her.

Without him close, a chilly emptiness seeped through her. Learning the extent of the hardships Matt had endured, knowing he'd trusted her enough to share his darkest memories with her created a new bond, a deeper intimacy between them. Being in his arms had felt so…right.

For a few minutes, Holly had believed he shared the sense of completeness she experienced in his embrace. Yet within a few seconds of stepping away from her, his manner changed. He composed himself, and the polite distance and protective shield he kept between them returned. Had she imagined the connection with him? Had the desire that pulsed to life in her veins been one-sided? Her instincts with people were usually much sharper, more accurate.

Matt shoved his hands in his pockets and rocked back on his heels. "Well, I know you've eaten, but I worked through lunch. I'm gonna go scrounge something in the kitchen."

"Sure," she said, still feeling a little numb, overwhelmed by everything Matt had revealed. "I, uh…fixed you a plate of leftover lasagna earlier if you want to reheat that. Or there's sliced ham for a sandwich, if you'd rather. Help yourself."

He gave her a grateful smile as he left the room, and Holly stood motionless for long minutes after he'd gone, replaying their conversation.

His wife's unfaithfulness, her suicide. Standing trial for murder. Watching everything he'd worked to build crumble and everyone he loved disappear from his life. So much taken from him. No wonder the burden had nearly broken him.

Nearly, but not entirely.

A spark of hope and pride in Matt flickered in her heart. Despite everything, he was coming back. He'd committed to pulling himself out of the quagmire of tragedy, dead set on fighting back and reclaiming what was rightfully his. Determined to do it on his own terms.

But when Matt rebuilt his old life, would there be any room in it for her?

Chapter 9

Matt stared blankly into the refrigerator, the draft cooling his skin as much as his memories chilled him inside. Holly had taken the news of his arrest much better than he'd expected. He'd been surprised that she didn't recognize his name. So much media attention had been drawn to his trial in Charlotte that his lawyer had argued for a change of venue. Which was how he ended up with Holly's husband prosecuting his case.

Even if his name didn't ring any bells now, he had no doubt recognition would dawn later. Then how would she feel toward him?

She'd said she cared about him, wanted to help him. But when she learned the full truth, everything would change. Perhaps that's why he'd withheld the last critical bit of information from her. He wasn't ready to see the suspicion and censure in her eyes. He wanted to steal just a few more moments of happiness with her. Because, dammit, he cared about her, too. He'd been so close to kissing her. The temptation had been strong, almost overwhelming.

He'd never met a woman as caring, as generous, as selfless as Holly. He'd never experienced the same crackle of attraction with another woman, even with Jill. Perhaps that had been part of his problem with his wife. Although he had loved Jill, he hadn't felt a fraction of the passion for her that he felt for Holly. When he was near Holly, his senses were sharper. He felt her presence to his marrow. When she was gone, her absence left him hollow, aching. He wanted to kiss her with every fiber of his being, but he knew doing so would be a mistake. One kiss from Holly would never be enough. And until she knew the full truth, how could he justify deepening the bond they shared? How could he take advantage of the desire that sparked between them when he knew the truth he kept from her could hurt her?

Soon enough, she'd share what he'd told her today with her brothers-in-law, and Matt's precarious house of cards would tumble. Until that time, he had to rein in his feelings for her. He had a duty to protect her from heartache, and that meant keeping an emotional distance between them. He would ignore the tug on his heart every time she smiled, squelch the heat that fired in his blood whenever they touched.

The way he saw it, he only had a few days left with her before the friendship they'd built caved under the weight of his deception. His sin of omission. Until that day came, he intended to give Holly the kind of joy and hope she'd imbued in him. He planned to make the holiday that she loved as special as he could. Maybe then, when she looked back on their time together, she would recall a few treasured moments.

And she'd forgive him.

The day after Thanksgiving, Holly woke to a dusting of snow on her lawn. The frosty weather put her in the perfect mood to start her Christmas celebrations. The first thing on her agenda was a hot breakfast for herself and Matt. Then she'd dive headfirst into transforming her home for the holidays. Every room would be decked in greenery and bows. Santa and his reindeer, angels and jolly elves would fill every nook, and the hand-painted porcelain nativity set she'd inherited from her great-grandmother would take center stage in her family room beside her tree. A live tree. No artificial tree would suffice.

A childlike enthusiasm and excitement kicked up her pulse as she hurried down the stairs, enticed by the scent of freshly brewed coffee.

When she reached the kitchen, Matt stood looking out her bay window at the new snow as he sipped from a steaming mug.

"Good morning," she said, a singsong quality ringing in her voice. "Beautiful day, isn't it? It's just perfect."

He lifted a corner of his mouth. "Perfect for what? Going back to bed?"

She gave him the raspberry and poured herself a large mug of coffee. "Perfect for picking out our Christmas tree." She scooped two large spoonfuls of sugar into her cup and stirred. "After breakfast, we can go into the woods behind the barn and cut down one of the Douglas firs."

"Cut down a Christmas tree?" Humor lit his gaze. "You're kidding, right?"

"Not a bit. I've had my eye on a couple for a few months that I think will be just the right size for the family room." She blew on her coffee to cool the edge before she sipped. "So are you game?"

He laughed, the sound as rich and full-bodied as her morning brew. "Your wish is my command."

She waved the spoon at him as if it were a magic wand. "I wish for you to help me turn my house into a Christmas wonderland today."

He arched an eyebrow. "No renovations?"

"Not today. Today is all about my favorite time of year."

"The after-Thanksgiving sales at the mall?" he asked, a teasing glint in his eyes.

She carried her mug over to join him at the window and socked him playfully in the arm. "Tease if you want, but by tonight, you'll see how serious I am about all things Christmas."

By the time Matt had cut down the fir tree Holly chose, his fingers were numb, and his ears and nose were frozen. But one look at the pure delight that sparkled in Holly's eyes as they'd hunted down the perfect Christmas tree warmed him from the inside out. The cold had turned her cheeks pink, and the lip gloss she'd dabbed on to protect her lips from the weather made her mouth all the more tempting.

After he tied the tree to the back of her ATV four-wheeler to drag back to the farmhouse, he turned to Holly. "All done. I don't know about you, but I'm ready to get back inside and thaw out."

She tipped her head toward the lightly falling snow, an expression of sheer joy lighting her face. A few flakes clung to her eyelashes and glinted like tiny diamonds. Matt had to call on every ounce of his willpower not to pull her close and sample the strawberry shimmer on her lips and touch her cheeks with his hands.

She hadn't mentioned their conversation from the day before, which suited him just fine. Resurrecting the black memories had been difficult enough without having to dwell on them to satisfy an endless string of questions.

He'd worried that she might feel awkward around him today, but if anything, their heart-to-heart had brought them closer. Matt savored the new depth to their friendship, the closeness, the connection, knowing how fragile that bond was. Spending time with Holly revived his belief that there was still good in the world, that happiness could be found in the simple pleasures. Fresh snow, an aromatic pine tree, a litter of playful kittens. She'd lost her husband to a brutal murder, yet she hadn't let tragedy defeat her. She'd persevered in the face of her grief and relished moments of joy wherever she found them.

Beyond the employment and shelter she'd offered him, her optimism and encouragement fed his hungry soul the hope and happiness he craved. For that, he owed her a tremendous debt of gratitude. And how did he repay her? Deception.

His gut twisted. She deserved so much better.

He ground his back teeth together in self-reproach as he revved the four-wheeler, ready to head back to the farmhouse. Holly swung a leg over the seat behind him and wrapped her arms around his chest to hold on. The press of her body sent a wave of heat sizzling through him.

They bounced their way over the roots and potholes, the wintery wind nipping their faces. Once home, Matt parked the ATV and helped Holly climb off. Before he could release her hand, she tugged him close and smiled up at him. "Thank you, Matt. I had fun. Cutting down a tree to decorate has been a tradition in my family for years, and it just wouldn't have felt like Christmas going to some lot to buy one."

She startled him with a quick kiss, nothing more than a friendly peck on his mouth, but the touch of her lips, the sweet taste of her lip gloss jolted him as if he'd touched a live power line.

His body on fire, he watched her greet Magic and her kittens, refilling their food bowl before she disappeared inside. Matt shook himself from the spell of her kiss and unlashed the fir tree from the back of the ATV. He hauled the fir to the family room while Holly heated a kettle of water for hot chocolate. When she brought him a steaming mug of cocoa, complete with tiny marshmallows, he chuckled.

"Palmer always loved to pile marshmallows in her hot chocolate."

She gave him a satisfied nod. "I can't blame her. Cocoa without marshmallows is just…" She waved a hand searching for the right word.

"Hot chocolate milk?" he suggested.

"Well, yeah! I was going to say it was un-American or a sacrilege or something. Cocoa *needs* marshmallows," she stated, a conviction blazing in her eyes as if she were arguing a deeply held political belief.

She punctuated her declaration by taking a sip of her drink and humming her satisfaction. Her pleasured sigh sang through his veins and conjured images of sweaty bodies tangled together in the throes of passion.

A sweet foam clung to her upper lip when she lowered her mug, and Matt's body quickened when she licked it off. His thoughts flashed back to their brief kiss, and he balled his hands at his sides to keep from reaching for her.

Holly lifted her mug in a salute. "I'm feeling warmer already."

He sent her a wry smile and averted his gaze. "Yeah, me, too."

She drank again then set her cup aside. "Okay, let's get to work. The tree stand is in that blue box. If you'll hold the tree straight, I'll wiggle underneath and screw it in."

Doing his best to ignore the many double entendres possible in her last statement, Matt nodded, downed another gulp of cocoa and retrieved the stand. Although he was trying to be a gentleman, trying to keep their friendship platonic, trying to protect her from a deeper involvement that could hurt her later, a man had his limits.

If she gave him so much as a hint that she wanted him as much as he hungered for her, all bets were off.

After they'd secured the tree in its stand, Holly filled the water trough and left the tree to soak up some hydration before they started decorating. Instead she turned her attention to arranging sprigs of holly with red bows on the mantel and winding pine garlands around the staircase banister.

Matt helped her pose the nativity figures and place Santa

memorabilia around the house. By evening, the house was filled with festive decorations and the savory scent of the beef stew she'd had simmering in her Crock-Pot.

She whipped up a batch of corn bread to go with the stew, and she and Matt ate their dinner by a crackling fire in the family room.

As she enjoyed her meal, Holly reflected on the day. Spending time with Matt, sharing her family traditions with him, had made the holiday preparations special.

Even knowing how much Christmas meant to her, Ryan had never helped her decorate the house like Matt had today. Ryan had always begged off, claiming he had too much work to finish for a case or swearing he couldn't possibly miss whatever football game was on TV. He'd indulged her Christmas fanaticism but rarely participated.

Sharing the decorating with someone this year had made the process infinitely more fun and memorable—a blessing, considering how lonely the holiday could have felt in the wake of Ryan's death. Last year, her first holiday season without him, had been empty and almost more than she could bear.

After cleaning up their dishes, Holly returned to the family room with fresh mugs of spiced cider and handed Matt a cup. Turning, she started one of her favorite Christmas CDs playing softly in the background. "A little mood music while we decorate the tree?"

Matt smiled warmly. "You really are a Christmas nut."

"I am the whole Christmas fruitcake when it comes to decorating and baking and keeping traditions like kissing under the mistletoe."

Matt arched an eyebrow. "Oh, you have mistletoe in that box? That's one holiday tradition I could get enthused about."

He waggled his eyebrows mischievously, and she laughed.

"I don't do fake mistletoe. We have to go back into the woods and collect some real mistletoe later."

He barked a laugh and shook his head. "And why didn't we

collect it this morning while we were already out freezing our butts off?"

She braced her hands on her hips and gave him a playful scowl. "So sue me. I forgot." She tipped her head and appraised him. "How are you at climbing trees?"

He lifted his eyebrows. "I have a better idea. Find me a BB gun, and I'll shoot some mistletoe down for you."

"Spoilsport." She jabbed his arm and laughed again. "Okay, lights first."

"Lights," he groaned. "I suppose you even like hanging the lights, tangles, burned-out bulbs and all?"

"I simplify things by keeping new strands of lights handy if anything goes wrong with the previous year's string. But yeah, I love the lights most. They're my favorite part of the tree."

She took one end of the coiled lights and began unwinding the cord as she draped twinkling lights on the evergreen branches. The pine scent of the tree filled her nose, and her spirits soared. Memories of decking the tree with her sisters flooded her mind, and she smiled to herself.

Then a fresh, soapy scent joined the aroma of pine, and Matt's arms reached around her to help secure the dangling strand of lights she juggled.

For weeks she'd worked beside Matt scraping, painting, hammering and sanding without losing her head, but the sentimentality of decorating her tree, the evocative smells and cherished memories associated with her holiday traditions left her emotions raw and vulnerable. His sexy scent made her lightheaded, and the brush of his chest against her back when he moved in close to assist her with a tangle of wires sent her own circuits haywire. His body heat enveloped her, both filling her with a deep-seated peace and security and making her pulse race. Holly didn't miss the significance of that dichotomy.

Kenny G's sultry saxophone playing in the background only heightened the heady romanticism of the moment. Holly was sure Matt could hear the thump of her heart as they worked their way around the tree, arranging the lights and securing the strands on the branches.

By the time they finished, her head spun, and her breathing had grown shallow and quick. She gulped a few restorative lungfuls of oxygen as she retrieved the first box of ornaments.

Matt cleared his throat. "Palmer and Miles would have loved this. All the decorating. Cutting down the tree." He paused, his eyes sad. "Did I tell you that I tried to call my kids yesterday?"

She caught her breath. "And?"

He shook his head. "Jill's mother answered. It got ugly fast, and when I tried to call back, no one answered. She probably unplugged the phone."

Holly sighed, her shoulders sloping. "Matt, I'm sorry. Don't give up. Things are turning around for you, and I know that in time, you'll get your children back, too."

"God, I hope so." He scrubbed a hand over his face and shook his head as if shaking off the serious mood. He pointed toward the storage box. "What ya got there?"

Holly popped the top off the plastic storage box and dug into the bubble-wrapped ornaments. Lifting out a couple, she handed one to Matt. "I've always felt like decorating the house was almost as much fun as opening gifts on Christmas morning."

He cocked his head as he peeled back the protective wrapping on the ornament she'd handed him. "How do you figure that?"

"Well…" She grinned and made a show of parting the wrappings from her bundle slowly and carefully. "Taking the decorations out of the storage box is a little like opening lots of tiny presents. And each decoration holds a special memory from when it was purchased or given as a gift. Every ornament has a story, a special meaning for me. It's like reliving Christmases past." She extracted a clear glass angel. "Take this one, for example. Ryan and I bought it on a shopping trip in Chattanooga when we were first married."

Matt glanced at the angel. "It's lovely." He held up the ornament he'd just unwrapped. "What's the story here? A birthday cake?"

"Ah, that is the oldest and most special ornament of all! My parents gave me that on my fifth birthday. See, I was born on December twenty-fourth—"

Matt's head came up, his expression reflecting surprise at this news.

"—and I was feeling a little forgotten in the shadow of all the Christmas activities that year. When I opened it, my dad told me my birthday could never be forgotten, because I was the best Christmas present he ever got."

When she paused, reflecting, Matt smiled. "And your name—Holly—"

"Is proof that my parents have a sense of humor. My full name is Holly *Noel* Bancroft Cole." She tapped *ba-dump-dum* with her hands on the top of one of the storage boxes like a drummer after a stand-up's joke, and Matt chuckled. "With a Christmas Eve birthday, how could I not love Christmas?"

"How indeed." Matt smiled and motioned toward the tree with the birthday cake ornament. "May I?"

"I'd be honored." She followed him and hung the glass angel on a top bough. Moving back to the box, she lifted out more hand-painted balls, lacy linen snowflakes and homemade clothespin reindeer. She was grinning to herself, remembering the lopsided aluminum foil star Zoey made one year for the top of the tree, when Matt's hand closed around hers. He tugged her into his arms, and when she gave him a curious look, he smiled. "Dance with me?"

Kenny G was playing a slow, sultry version of "Have Yourself A Merry Little Christmas" from her speakers, and as the evening darkened outside, the twinkling of lights from the tree cast the family room in a golden glow. The moment had a fairy-tale quality, and when Matt pulled her into his arms, Holly's breath rushed from her lungs. His hand settled at the base of her spine as he took the first shuffling steps of a slow dance, and a sweet tingling raced over her skin.

She placed her free hand on his shoulder, moving stiffly in his embrace. Her head struggled past the awkwardness of their employer/employee relationship, but her heart lunged full speed into this new intimacy. Holly's pulse pounded in her head, drowning out all but the sweet, low humming near her ear as Matt accompanied the sax on the CD. She swayed slowly with him, snuggling closer with each step, until her body pressed against his. Matt stroked her spine, stirring a flurry of sensation low in her belly. Her body throbbed as dormant desires pulsed through her blood. The steady drum of his heart next to hers reverberated through her chest. She clutched the soft cotton of his flannel shirt at his back and nestled her head on his shoulder. Matt's sexy scent, his warm embrace, his strength surrounded her, flowed through her, intoxicated her.

As they danced across her floor, she couldn't imagine anywhere else she'd rather be at that moment. With Matt she'd found a comfort and happiness she hadn't known in a long time.

As the song ended, far too soon for Holly's liking, she leaned back to glance up at his face, admiring the rugged angles highlighted by the warm lights of the Christmas tree. His eyes met hers and heated.

When he traced the curve of her jaw with a crooked knuckle, she tipped her head, savoring his gentle caress and sighing her contentment with the peaceful moment.

His hand slid to her chin, and he angled her face toward his. Moved closer. His intent blazed in his eyes, and Holly could only hold her breath in anticipation as he dipped his head.

Chapter 10

When Matt pressed his lips tenderly against hers, his kiss sizzled through her. With a mewl of approval, she rose on her toes to deepen their embrace. Her arms tightened around him, encouraging him, and she slid her fingers up his spine into his thick hair.

"Holly," he rasped as he cupped his palms against her cheeks and angled his head for a deeper kiss. A rumble of satisfaction issued from his throat when she swept her tongue into his mouth to duel with his. The heavy beat that her heart had pounded as they danced now thundered, shaking her to the core. Her skin flushed hot, and a coil of desire tightened inside her.

She tasted the cinnamon and cloves of the spiced cider on his lips and longed to savor Matt's kiss for hours.

But the jarring ring of her phone jangled from the kitchen. Startled, she gasped as she jerked back from his embrace. She lifted a hand to her chest, as if she could muffle the staccato pulse of her racing heart, and gave him an apologetic look.

She didn't want to move, didn't want to talk to anyone. She wanted only to step back into Matt's arms and continue the heavenly kiss.

Later she would analyze what this turn in their relationship meant, where they might be heading, what she was supposed to do with her growing feelings for Matt. Right now, she only wanted to feel. Because with Matt, she felt more alive, more hopeful, more at peace than she had since the sheriff's deputy arrived at her door to inform her Ryan's body had been found in an abandoned church in town.

The harsh ringing continued, and Matt stroked her cheek, a resigned expression tempering the heat in his gaze. "Maybe you should get that. It could be important."

"Not as important as what we were doing." She leaned into him, squeezing a handful of his shirt and brushing a soft kiss along his jaw. And knowing the magical, impulsive moment had passed.

Matt tugged up the corner of his mouth in his heart-stopping lopsided grin. "I'll be here when you get back."

He stepped away and pulled another ornament from the box to hang on the tree.

The incessant ring of her phone continued, and with a sigh, Holly trotted into the kitchen to answer the annoying summons. "Hello?"

"Have you heard anything from Zoey?" her older sister said without preamble or greeting.

Holly chuckled. "And hello to you, too, Paige."

"Well, have you?"

Hearing the distress in her sister's voice, Holly sobered. "Should I have?"

"Well, I was hoping—Holly, she took off a few days ago, and we haven't heard from her. She and Dad had a fight about…oh, something. I don't know. You know how Zoey is, how reckless and impulsive she can be. We've called and called, but she doesn't answer her cell. We're really getting worried about her."

Holly sank down onto a kitchen chair and raked her fingers

through her hair. "You don't have any idea where she's gone? She's not at any of her friends' houses?"

"We've tried everyone we can think of, even her friend Gage Powell. I was hoping that maybe she'd gone up there to stay with you." Paige, who could normally be relied on to keep a cool head, sounded at her wit's end. "Please tell me she's called you."

"I wish I could." Holly racked her brain, searching for some new possibility to offer concerning her younger sister's whereabouts. Zoey had always been impulsive, impractical and a bit of a drama queen, but it wasn't like her to take off without being in communication with someone in the family. Holly hoped that when Zoey had had a chance to calm down a bit, she would call one of her older sisters. "You don't have any idea what the fight was about?"

"Dad said something about her new boyfriend. I don't think he likes the guy much."

Holly rolled her eyes. "So what else is new? When has Dad ever liked the men we choose?"

"He liked Ryan."

"I think Ryan just grew on him after a while. When I first brought him home, Ryan was just that guy who was stealing his daughter. You know Dad. Nobody is good enough for his daughters."

"Well…I think he likes Brent. Correction, he loves Brent."

Holly heard her sister sigh and wondered if the fatigue she heard in her sister's voice could be completely attributed to Zoey's disappearance. "Try not to worry too much about Zoey. She's a big girl, and even though she's flaky at times, she knows how to take care of herself. I'll let you know if I hear from her. In the meantime, you take care of yourself, Paige. Don't wear yourself out, planning this wedding and trying to be Ms. Perfect."

"I'm not—" Paige stopped abruptly and gave a short humorless laugh. "Okay, so maybe I am. I just want this wedding to be—"

"Perfect?" Holly asked, smiling.

Paige huffed, and Holly could picture her sister scowling. The only thing Paige hated more than imperfection, was being teased for her perfectionism. "You'll let us know if you hear from Zoey?"

"Of course." Holly finished her call with her sister and made her way back to the family room, where Matt was still decorating the tree.

He took one look at her face and asked, "Something wrong?"

"My sister Zoey took off, and Paige hasn't heard from her. She's worried and wanted to know if I'd heard from her." Holly bit her bottom lip and furrowed her brow. "I tried to reassure Paige, but I have to admit, Zoey taking off like this has me worried, too. It's a bit rash, even for Zoey. Apparently she had a fight with my dad a few days ago, and no one has heard from her since."

Matt slid the loop at the top of a pinecone angel on a bough and gave Holly a sympathetic look. "You're close to your sisters, aren't you?"

"Yes. Not as close now as I was when we were in high school. Sometimes I feel a bit isolated from my family living so far away from them. But we talk by phone, as often as possible. I guess that's why Zoey's disappearance bothers me. I'd have thought she'd call me, to complain about the fight with Dad, if nothing else. But she hasn't."

"Anything I can do?" Matt stepped toward her, and the compassion in his eyes burrowed deep and stirred a warmth in Holly's chest.

She shook her head and gave him a forlorn smile. "Help me put the star on top? I'm too short without a ladder."

"Sure."

Holly brushed the protective packing materials away from her heirloom tree-topper and offered it to him. She stepped back for a better view, helping with verbal directions until the star was straight, then taking in the beauty of the finished product.

Matt joined her, and sliding an arm around her shoulders, he appraised their handiwork. "Not bad."

She grunted and elbowed him in the ribs. "Not bad? It's beautiful!"

He chuckled and kissed the top of her head. "Yeah, it is. And so are you."

Holly's breath caught. She angled her head to look up at him, not certain she'd heard him right. But the desire and affection that glowed in his eyes told her she hadn't imagined his compliment. An answering heat sluiced through her.

Matt slid an arm to her waist and drew her closer. Every place her body brushed his, her nerve endings crackled and her blood seemed to thicken, pulsing heavily through her veins.

"Now…where were we?" he asked, his voice dipping low in seductive tones.

"About right here." Holly tunneled her fingers into his hair, capturing his head and rising on her toes to caress his lips with hers.

A rumble of pleasure reverberated deep in his chest, and Holly absorbed the vibrations as she pressed closer, leaning into their kiss. His hand skated from the small of her back to cup her bottom, pulling her hips flush with his—and the hard ridge that telegraphed his desire for her.

She'd shared so much of herself with Matt in the past weeks. Her home. Her hopes. Her heartaches. But that superficial connection wasn't enough anymore. She craved something deeper, more personal, more intimate. A clamoring need flashed through her—to feel his skin on hers, to have his hands stroking her, to take him inside her.

She tugged his shirt free from his jeans. When she skimmed her hands beneath the fabric and over the width of his warm bare back, he tensed and hissed through his teeth. Pulling back from their kiss, she raised a querying look.

He tugged one cheek up in a lopsided grin. "Your hands are cold."

Holly bit her lip. "Sorry."

He nudged her chin up for another kiss. "Don't worry. We'll warm them up."

Without warning, he caught her behind the knees with one arm and swept her off her feet. Cradling her in his arms, he headed for the stairs.

Holly's pulse throbbed, and her body hummed with anticipation.

"If this isn't what you want—" he said, climbing the steps two at a time, "—tell me."

Holly entertained only the briefest image of Ryan in her head, before shoving it aside and focusing on the blue fire in Matt's loving gaze.

Ryan was her past.

Matt was the present. Here and now. Heat and desire. A chance to move forward.

In answer, she fingered open the top button of his shirt, then the next. "I still have condoms in my bedside stand we can use."

He nodded. "Perfect."

Instead of her bedroom, Matt carried her to his guest room and set her feet on the floor.

"Wait here. I'll be right back."

While he retrieved the condoms, her attention gravitated to the queen-size bed where the sheets were still unmade and rumpled from his night's sleep. A fresh wave of tingling expectation coursed through her.

Matt was back in seconds, tossing a couple foil packets on the bed and pulling her back into his arms. He dipped his head and kissed her deeply. As his tongue danced with hers, her knees trembled so hard, she had to lean into him for support.

Holly dug her fingers into the corded muscles of his arms, straining nearer, savoring every sweet stroke of his restless hands on her back, her bottom, her arms. Finally, he pulled at her sweater, and with sure hands, he dragged the soft top up and off, helping her free her arms from the long sleeves.

The cool nip of air on her overheated skin heightened her anticipation, and her nipples beaded beneath her plain, white satin bra. He raked an appreciative gaze over her, his eyes darkening to the navy shade of the sky at dusk. His hands molded and shaped her breasts, thumbing the peaks before he pressed openmouthed kisses to the upper swell at the edge of her bra.

This time when her knees buckled, they tumbled together onto his bed, and the weight of his body covering her kicked her senses into overdrive. Holly wrapped her legs around Matt's hips, angling her body to rub against his groin. Hot sparks flashed through her, coalescing in her womb, and another groan of satisfaction rumbled in Matt's throat.

He dragged the straps of her bra down and thumbed the front clasp open with finesse. Shoving the bra out of his way, Matt kissed his way across her bare breast until he covered the nipple with the heat of his mouth. His tongue lashed her sensitive flesh, shooting pure pleasure through her. He treated her other breast to the ministrations of nimble fingers, plucking, rolling and massaging her. The sizzling need built, and she arched her back, offering fuller access to his questing hands.

Not bothering with the rest of his buttons, Holly bunched his shirt in her palms and dragged it over his head, exposing the expanse of his chest to her exploration. Soon his pants and hers followed the other discarded clothes to the floor. She slid along his naked body, glorying in the sensual feel of warm skin on skin, the glide of his muscled angles against her soft curves. The contact drove her closer to the edge of control. Her body shook, ready to fly apart at any moment.

But Matt wasn't ready to give her the climax of which she teetered on the edge. He backed off the frenzied pace, the flurry of hands and mouths and intertwined bodies.

"Matt, now…please," she rasped, clinging to him and raining kisses along his throat and chin.

"There's no rush," he whispered, brushing his lips over the shell of her ear with butterfly strokes. "I want to savor you, memorize every detail of how you look, how you feel."

His fingers drew lazy circles on her hip, around her navel, down to her thigh. She sucked in a sharp breath as his hand skimmed over her bottom and the small of her back. A tiny whimper, half impatience, half pleasure escaped her throat. His kisses followed a similar leisurely tour of her body, teasing and enticing and bringing her to higher levels of sensation than she'd ever known.

Surrendering to his slower pace, she explored every tempting inch of his taut skin. When he'd moan his enjoyment, she'd catalog the erogenous spot for future reference then nibble and caress the sensitive point until he, too, trembled with need. The curve of his throat. The tip of his hip bone. The palm of his hand.

When they'd endured all of the sweet torture they could, he retrieved a condom, sheathed himself and settled between her legs. With a slow, sensual thrust, he joined their bodies, their souls. The rhythmic motion of their coupling built the drumming pulse inside her, wound the need tighter, until she shattered in a sweet oblivion.

"Holly…" he whispered, his lips pressed to her ear, as his body shuddered and his arms tightened around her. "Precious Holly."

Neither of them moved for long moments afterward. His breath, sawing raggedly in her ear, calmed, and her scampering pulse steadied.

The sun had long ago faded outside, leaving the guest room completely dark, when Matt whispered, "Stay with me tonight."

The choice was easy. She wasn't nearly ready to leave the warmth, the bliss she'd found in his arms.

She could wait until morning to face the inevitable questions of where their relationship would go from here. For now, she was at peace.

* * *

Matt stared into the inky darkness, Holly's heartbeat a steady bumping against his chest as she lay in his arms. Recriminations nipped at his thoughts like a vicious little dog biting his ankles.

He should have been completely honest with her before they'd slept together. He'd taken advantage of her trust. She deserved to know the truth about his connection to her late husband.

Guilt and regret slid through him, souring the sweet joy of making love to Holly.

He'd blown his best chance to level with her, and now he stood a greater chance of hurting her when he told her the truth, when he exposed his deception.

And he had no choice now. He had to come clean with her.

They'd moved their relationship to a new level, and he had a moral obligation to give her all the facts. He was overdue giving her the truth.

Matt buried his nose in her hair and inhaled the intoxicating herbal scent of her shampoo. She stirred as she slept, and he kissed her temple, quieted her with a stroke of his palm over her bare shoulder.

He'd been wrong to invest so much of himself in Holly. He had no right to think they had a future together when he had nothing to offer her. When he couldn't even tell her the truth of who he was.

Pain sliced through him and tangled with the warmth Holly had planted in his heart. He had no one to blame but himself for the heartache he knew would come. He'd wronged the woman he was falling in love with.

When Holly learned the whole truth about his past, he prayed she could find a way to forgive him.

Chapter 11

Holly drifted through the next couple of days on cloud nine. When she was at school, her thoughts strayed frequently to Matt, and she looked forward to fireside dinners with him and long nights in each other's arms.

When he seemed distant or troubled at times, she excused his pensive reticence. The whirlwind pace of their relationship sometimes had her stepping back to catch her breath, as well. But she relished the rush of excitement, the exhilaration of their deepening relationship. The growing bond she had with Matt felt…right.

Late that week, while she was putting the finishing touches on dinner and Matt was outside gathering wood to build a fire, a loud knocking jarred her out of a cheery verse of "We Wish You A Merry Christmas." Still humming under her breath, Holly answered her door and found Robert, in uniform, standing on her front porch. He gave her an uneasy look, his hands shoved in his back pockets. "Can we talk?"

Still unwilling to dismiss the disaster of Thanksgiving, she folded her arms over her chest. "About what?"

Robert nodded his head toward the door. "May I come in?"

Stepping back, she let him inside. As she led him into the family room, Holly reminded herself that this was Ryan's family. For Ryan's sake, she took a deep breath and battled down the resentment that bubbled inside. "Can I get you something to drink?"

He pulled off his gloves and pocketed them. "Sure."

He followed her into the kitchen, and when she opened the refrigerator, he glanced over her shoulder. "What time is it?"

She gave him a puzzled frown and flipped her wrist to check her watch. "Ten after six."

"Good, then I'm off duty." He reached past her and snagged a beer from the top shelf.

"I don't think—" Holly began, knowing alcohol wouldn't help the conversation she needed to have with Robert, but he'd already popped the cap and taken a swig.

With a sigh of resignation, she swallowed the rest of her argument as she pulled out a diet cola for herself.

As they strolled into her family room, Robert glanced around at her decorations and smiled. "The place looks nice. You've been busy."

Holly took a seat in a chair across from Robert. "Thank you. Matt helped me."

Her brother-in-law stiffened slightly when she mentioned Matt's name. "Actually, Rankin is the reason I'm here. I wanted to apologize for my behavior the other day. You were a guest in my home, and I didn't make you feel welcome."

Holly shifted in her seat and eyed Robert. "I'm not worried about me. Families have disagreements from time to time. You get over it and move on. But you invaded the privacy of somebody that I care about. You went behind my back and abused the power of your position trying to dig up dirt on somebody who's been nothing but kind and helpful to me.

Your intrusion was uncalled-for. That's what you should be apologizing for."

Robert squared his shoulders as a muscle in his jaw twitched. "Did you ask him about his name? Did you ask him why there's no record of his past?"

Holly lifted her chin. "I did."

Robert arched an eyebrow and took a sip of his drink. "And?"

"He changed his name three years ago, unofficially, because his real name had been dragged through the mud. He was looking for a clean start."

Narrowing his eyes, Robert leaned forward and braced his arms on his knees, letting his beer bottle dangle from his fingers. "So who is he? What's his real name?"

"Matt Randall. He's a pediatrician who practiced in Charlotte until his wife committed suicide several years ago. Because of circumstantial evidence, he was accused of killing her."

Color drained from Robert's face. "My God."

Holly raised a hand to silence the argument she knew was coming. "He didn't do it. The jury saw through the flimsy evidence and acquitted him. But by then the damage to his reputation had been done. He'd lost his practice, and his in-laws sued him for custody of his children."

Robert shifted his gaze to stare blankly at Holly's Christmas tree. His stunned expression and the furrow in his brow told Holly he was deep in thought.

"He moved to Morgan Hollow to find work. He's been punishing himself for everything that happened, sending all of his money to his children, virtually living on the streets as some form of penance. He feels guilty about his wife's death. He thinks he should have seen the signs and stopped her."

Setting his beer aside, Robert rubbed his chin and turned an incredulous look toward Holly. "Matt Randall?"

Holly frowned. "Yes. Why?"

He cocked his head and sent her a speculative glare. "Does that name not ring a bell for you?"

Her pulse tripped. "Should it?"

"Oh, yeah. It should."

"He said his case received a lot of media attention in Charlotte, and the venue had to be changed. Is that what you mean?"

"Did he tell you which venue the case was changed to?"

Robert's calculating expression triggered alarms inside her. "What's going on, Robert? What aren't you telling me?"

"Jon said he thought he recognized Rankin, and now I know why. I remember his case. I remember well, because Ryan told me how frustrating the case was."

"*Ryan* told you? What are you talking about?" Holly's nerves jangled.

"So Rankin—or should I say Randall—didn't tell you the best part?"

Robert's self-satisfied smile nettled her. Oxygen backed up in her lungs, and, somehow, she knew what he was going to say before he said it.

"The Randall murder was Ryan's case. Your husband prosecuted Matt Randall for murder."

A fist of shock squeezed Holly's lungs, and she struggled to breathe. Denials rang in her head. Matt wouldn't have kept something so critically important from her. Would he?

But Robert's confident expression assured her that Matt had deceived her. A gnawing disillusionment and betrayal bit her gut.

"There…must be some…explanation," she fumbled.

Robert folded his arms over his chest and scoffed. "Oh, I'm sure there is. I'm just not sure it's a reason you want to hear. Jon and I tried to warn you Rankin wasn't who he said, that you shouldn't trust him."

Holly dug her fingers into the seat cushion and sucked in a shaky breath. Her mind buzzed numbly as she tried to sort out the shocking truths Robert had tossed at her feet. "I just can't believe…."

"Oh, come on, Holly! Wake up and smell the horse manure

this guy has been shoveling at you!" Robert shoved to his feet, gaping at her. As he stared at her, his expression morphed from disbelief to enlightenment, and his eyes widened. "Hell, Holly, you told Jon that the day you met him, Rankin followed you into the church where Ryan was killed."

A chill slithered down her spine. "S-so?"

Robert spread his hands and raised his eyebrows as if the rest of his thought process should be obvious. "He sought you out. Has it occurred to you that maybe he had an ulterior motive?"

"A motive?" The sinister turn of the conversation flooded her stomach with acid.

"Retribution maybe? Revenge against the man who prosecuted him?"

Holly could barely speak. Dread and disillusionment knotted her throat. "But Ryan is dead."

Robert waved her denial away. "So he goes after Ryan's widow…poetic justice."

She shook her head vehemently, unable to accept Matt could be so vindictive. "He wouldn't do that. Matt isn't like that."

"Are you sure? Are you really willing to bet your life on it?" Robert shoved his hands in his pockets and glowered at her. Then his expression shifted again, and he stiffened his spine. "Dear God, Holly, the man is a vagrant."

"No." Ice sluiced through her veins. Holly held up a hand and paced to the far side of the room, not wanting to hear Robert's theory, knowing where his reasoning was headed. "He had a job, had an inexpensive place to live, he wasn't homeless."

"He moved to Morgan Hollow right after he was acquitted—"

"To take a construction job, not to track down Ryan!"

Even as justifications and denials sprang from her lips, she remembered the watch Matt had that looked just like Ryan's, and she questioned his silence about Ryan's part in his prosecution. What else might Matt be hiding from her?

Tears filled her eyes, and a searing pain slashed through her chest.

"He had the means, the opportunity and a motive, Holly. In my line of work, coincidences usually aren't coincidences. You have to be realistic. I know this guy has swindled you with his charm and good looks, but—"

Holly bristled. "Stop!"

Fury blazed through her veins—toward Robert…and herself. Because there was a grain of truth to his insinuation. She had fallen for Matt's warmth and sex appeal. She'd excused his earlier reticence, then when he had finally opened up, she'd believed every word he had told her about his past without reservation. But how much of what he said was true? Had he played on her emotions?

Robert sent her a sympathetic look. "I know this has all been a shock to you, but now that you know the truth, you have no excuse to keep him around. In fact, we have every reason to look more closely at exactly who Randall is and why he's here."

Holly sank slowly to her chair, trembling to her core. Before she could respond to Robert, she heard the back door open and heavy footsteps approaching the family room.

"Holly, I brought in some firewood. It's getting cold out there, and I thought—" Matt stopped midsentence when he entered the room and spotted Robert.

Robert folded his arms across his chest and narrowed a glare on Matt. "Well, speak of the devil."

Matt took one look at Holly's reddened eyes and stricken expression, and his heart clenched. "Holly, what's wrong? What's happened?"

All forms of disaster and tragedy whirled through his mind, but as soon as he glimpsed the accusation burning in Robert's eyes, Matt knew all he needed. Her brother-in-law had learned his true identity, made the connection to Ryan and shared his deception with Holly.

His heart sank, and self-reproach sawed in his gut. He'd had his chance to tell her the truth and foolishly postponed the inevitable.

Moving stiffly, he laid the split logs in the fireplace and dusted off his hands. When he faced the room again, both Holly and her brother-in-law stared at him silently. Robert's expression was contemptuous. Holly's face reflected deep hurt and betrayal.

With guilt and regret settling like rocks in his chest, Matt took a slow, deep breath. "Holly, I'm sorry. I'd planned to tell you, but—"

"Robert, if you don't mind, I'd like you to go now." She spoke to her brother-in-law, but her eyes held Matt's. The pain and questions filling her gaze gouged his soul.

"Actually, I do mind. I have a few questions for Randall."

Holly snapped a piercing, pleading gaze toward Robert. "Later. I want to talk to Matt first." When her brother-in-law still didn't move, she added, "Alone."

Robert shook his head. "I don't think that's a good idea."

She drew herself up, her petite frame rigid. "I didn't ask for your opinion." Then softening her tone, she whispered, "Please. Just leave."

Taking his beer from the coffee table, Robert drank deeply and divided a weighty, distrusting stare between Matt and Holly. When the bottle was empty, he thunked it down and stalked to the door. "I'll check in with you later." He sent Matt a dark scowl before glancing back at Holly. "Be careful."

Robert slammed the door behind him, and the bang echoed through the house.

His heart heavy and guilt pounding in his head, Matt faced Holly. "I can explain. I know it looks bad, but—"

"Did you kill my husband?" she rasped.

Her question punched him in the gut like a physical blow. "What! Is that what he told you?"

"Answer the question!" Her hands fisted at her sides, and

her body vibrated with fury. Tears mingled with sparks of anger in her eyes, and her suspicion slashed a deep gash in his soul. Did she really believe he was capable of murder?

"No." His tone was firm, resolute. He met her accusing gaze with an unflinching stare.

Holly squeezed her eyes shut, and two fat tears trickled down her cheeks.

Matt took a step toward her, needing to touch her, needing to hold her and reassure her. Needing to reestablish the bond they'd shared over the past several days. But she tensed when he moved, and the hot glare she shot him warned him away.

Her brow furrowed, and she shook her head. "When were you going to tell me?"

"Soon. I—"

"But not before you'd slept with me first."

The bitterness behind her words chafed, sending another arrow of self-reproach to his marrow.

"I should have told you before we made love. I know that. I intended—"

"Love?" She barked a mirthless laugh. "How can you use that word when you've been lying to me from the very start? You've known all along who I was, who Ryan was. Haven't you?"

Matt gritted his teeth, knowing she deserved the hard truth and hating the sour taste of it. He'd betrayed her trust and deserved her anger. More than anything, he wanted to avoid hurting Holly, but he'd done exactly that with his evasiveness and silence.

"I figured it out the day we brought the stained glass home for you."

"Is that why you sought me out at the old church? Were you planning some sort of revenge against Ryan through me?"

"Revenge? No! Of course not. And I didn't realize who you were until I saw the picture of you and Ryan by your bed when you took me to see the renovations needed in the master bathroom."

"But you didn't say anything then. Why?"

He huffed his frustration, suddenly bone-tired. "I should have. I know I should have. I'm sorry I didn't, Holly. But by then I'd promised to help you with your renovations and…honestly, I was still in shock, trying to figure out what I needed to do. I needed the work. I wanted to work for you, but I was afraid if you knew who I was…"

When he hesitated, she spread her hands. "That I wouldn't hire you? That I'd believe you were guilty? That I wouldn't give you a fair chance to tell your side of things?" Her tone was rife with exasperation and hurt.

"Yes!" he shouted, his own frustration mounting. "I thought you'd judge me the way everyone else has judged me for five years. I thought you'd find me guilty because your husband had, and that I'd lose the friendship you were offering."

"So instead you lied to me?"

He rubbed the back of his neck. "Maybe by omission. But everything I have told you about what happened has been the truth."

"How do I know that?" She swiped at a tear that escaped her lashes, and the ache in his heart dug deeper. "How can I believe anything you've told me is the truth?"

For several moments he said nothing, fighting the urge that clawed inside him to pull her into his arms and kiss away the pain in her eyes. But he couldn't. Because he'd caused the hurt that she was suffering. Because with his deception, he'd broken the gossamer bond of friendship they'd formed.

Because she didn't belong to him and never had.

Finally, dragging in a fortifying breath, he said softly, "If life allowed us do-overs, Holly, there are a lot of things I'd do differently the second time around. I'd be a better husband to Jill. I'd not touch the evidence of Jill's suicide and incriminate myself." He paused, stepping closer and meeting her gaze. He tried with his tone, his expression, to convey all the sincerity and conviction that filled his heart. "But at the top of that list would be how I've handled things with you. Because the last thing I wanted was to hurt you. You've become very special to me. I care about you. Deeply. I hate the fact that my bad decisions have wounded you, have betrayed the trust you had in me. I wish to God I'd told you the truth from the start. But I was a coward." Her expression softened, and he harbored a hope that he was reaching her. "I saw something in you that I wanted, that I needed in my life. Your faith in me has revived my faith in myself. Your smiles have given me the first real joy I've had in years."

Suddenly, as if she'd been recalled to her senses, she jerked her chin up, and her eyes grew icy. "And let's not forget the sex. I've given you a few good rolls in the sack."

He flinched as if she'd slapped him. "Holly, don't...." He swallowed the knot of emotion that rose in his throat. "Please don't diminish what we've shared together. That was real. It was honest. It was about two people who cared about each other, and—"

"It was a mistake," she grated. "You used me."

"No!" he ground through clenched teeth, his voice breaking. "Holly, I'm sorry I didn't tell you about my connection to Ryan, but nothing else that has happened between us has been a lie! We have something special. Don't throw that away."

A cool detachment and resignation settled in her expression that worried him far more than her fiery anger and bitter hurt. "I'm not throwing it away. You did."

Like a candle snuffed out by an arctic blast, the last glimmer of Matt's hope that he could fix things with Holly sputtered out. His insides ache with a raw emptiness and chilling loss.

She aimed a finger at the door, her jaw set and firm. "Get out."

Turning on his heel, Matt gathered the shreds of his tattered soul and left the farmhouse. But he left his heart with Holly.

Chapter 12

Holly dragged through the next couple of days, unable to enjoy anything about the holiday season she usually loved. Every aspect of her Christmas celebrations had been tainted by memories of Matt. The decorations they'd hung together. The music they'd danced to. The cookies and eggnog they'd prepared.

She felt as if she'd been scraped raw inside. His dishonesty and deception cut a wide swath that wouldn't heal anytime soon. Because she'd let herself fall in love with Matt. Even the biting truth about his evasion and deceit didn't dampen the tender affection she'd developed for him. His absence left her hollow and aching. She missed his warm smiles across the breakfast table, the low melody of his voice when he sang in the shower, his reassuring presence when the winter nights loomed cold and empty.

When Paige called on Sunday night, Holly tried to sound upbeat, despite the heaviness in her heart. She didn't want Paige or the rest of her family needlessly worrying about her.

Her sister and parents had enough to worry about with Zoey's disappearance.

"I've decided to postpone my wedding," Paige announced after Holly told her that, no, she still hadn't heard from Zoey.

Holly gripped the phone tighter. "Postpone it? Why? For how long?"

"Indefinitely. I can't get married without Zoey there. Once we find her and bring her home, I'll reschedule."

She raked her hair back from her eyes, staggered by Paige's decision. "What did Brent say about waiting?"

"He's fine with it. In fact, Dad is thinking of sending Brent overseas to work on a new deal with some European investors. Once that deal is settled and he's back stateside, we'll set a new date." Rather than sounding disappointed about the delay, Paige sounded almost…relieved. "Holly, are you okay? You don't sound like yourself."

Blowing out a sigh, she flopped back on her sofa cushions and stared up at her ceiling. She should have expected Paige to pick up on her mood. Her sister was too perceptive, knew her too well.

"I'll be all right. Matt didn't turn out to be the man I'd thought he was. I kicked him out." Holly explained in vague terms about Matt's history, the truths he'd withheld from her, and Paige sympathized and consoled her as best she could.

"If I were there now I'd give you a big bear hug, honey. But, you know, I have to wonder…" Paige paused, and Holly could almost hear the wheels in her logical sister's brain turning. "Do you really think he kept his connection to Ryan a secret out of malice? Once he knew you well enough to confide in you, he told you everything else, as bleak and painful as the rest of his past was. That shows a special level of trust and faith."

Holly scoffed. "If he trusted me so much, then why didn't he tell me about Ryan prosecuting his case? That's a pretty important piece of the whole picture."

"True. But can you see how difficult, how awkward it would have been for him? Regardless of how you feel about his choice, can you blame him for wanting to build your friend-ship before dropping that bomb?"

Holly sat up on the couch, frowning. "Whose side are you on?"

"Yours, of course. But I'm trying to see his side. Trying to be fair."

Good old rational, practical Paige, weighing everything before deciding anything.

Holly plucked at a loose string on a throw draped over the back of her sofa. Had she overreacted to Matt's news? Had she let her initial hurt and anger sway her actions unfairly?

Her pain was still too new to have that perspective yet.

She caught up with Paige on other news from back home about Bancroft Industries, her parents' upcoming holiday party and the chat she'd had with their high school pal, Gage Powell, when she called him about Zoey's disappearance. By the time she hung up, Holly was suffering a bout of homesickness and opted for a warm bubble bath before bed.

After a long, lonely weekend and a longer, distracted Monday at school, she arrived home the next afternoon to find her front door unlocked and the lights on upstairs. She tensed and racked her brain to remember if Jon had mentioned working on her renovations today. After dumping her purse and coat in the foyer, she walked upstairs with her heart in her throat. She followed the sound of water running, edging toward her master bathroom. "Jon? Is that you?"

The water cut off, and a tall figure, splattered with paint, stepped through the bathroom door. "Oh, hi. I thought I heard someone."

Matt. Not Jon.

The sweet sight of him made her heart leap, followed quickly by a rush of heat as renewed anger flashed through her blood. "What are you doing here?"

He leveled his shoulders, his expression open, calm. "You hired me to finish your renovations, so I'm working. I've almost finished sponge painting in here if you want to see. I'm not sure this is turning out the way you envisioned."

She narrowed a disgruntled glare on him. "The other day, I asked you to leave."

His chin lifted, and hurt flashed over his face. "I recall. And I've moved my things out of the guest room today. But I made a commitment to you to help you finish the house by Christmas, and that's a promise I intend to keep."

She gaped at him, torn by the emotional tug-of-war inside her. Dedication to his commitments was exactly what she'd have expected from Matt—before Friday when she learned he'd kept her in the dark about such a critical piece of his past.

She shifted her weight nervously, fighting the tears of relief that stung her eyes. She *couldn't* be glad to see him after he'd so blatantly betrayed her trust. "How…how did you get here?"

"Taxi."

She grunted and shook her head. "You can't take a taxi back and forth from town every day! It'd cost a fortune."

He raised a palm. "I'd say that's my problem. How else am I supposed to get here?"

She bit her tongue to keep from offering to drive him—or rescind her eviction—even though the lift in his dark eyebrow hinted he thought she might.

She crossed her arms over her chest. "Maybe I don't want you coming out here at all."

His brow furrowed. "You're firing me?"

"I—" She caught herself. Floundered. Sent him a churlish scowl. "I should!"

The corner of his mouth dared to twitch. "But you're not."

She glared at him, the ache in her chest almost suffocating. "No. But stay out of my way. You can work while I'm at school, and our paths won't have to cross."

Disappointment dimmed his eyes, and he blew out a sigh. "You're the boss."

With that, she should have turned to leave, left him to his

task. But she couldn't make her feet move. When she continued staring at him, knowing all her tangled emotions were written on her face, he motioned to the bathroom.

"Wanna have a look?"

Curiosity spurred her to step into the master bath and check his progress. The lacy-looking maroon sponge pattern on her wall exceeded her expectations, and her breath caught.

Matt winced. "That bad? I knew I was too heavy-handed. Well…I can paint over what I've done and start again tomorrow, if you want."

"No, it looks great. I—" His shoulder brushed hers in the tight confines, and a tingling heat rushed through her. She stepped away from him, rubbing the goose bumps that rose on her arms.

"Holly—"

The husky, intimate pitch of his voice told her she didn't want to start the conversation he intended.

She hurried out to the bedroom, pausing only briefly at the door. "When you finish in here, I think you should go. Tomorrow, I'd prefer you finished before I got home from school."

But the next day, when she arrived at the farmhouse after an exhausting day with a room full of Christmas-crazed kindergartners, not only was Matt still there, but Jon was with him. She found the men upstairs, removing the old bathtub in the master bath.

Jon gave her a nod of acknowledgment when she poked her head around the corner and wiped his hands on the seat of his jeans. "We're almost finished, and I've got to be heading out." He looked at Matt. "Can you wrap things up here?"

Holly sent a quick glance to Matt, who looked sexier than he should have with his hair mussed, a smudge of something black on his cheek and a sheen of perspiration on his brow. She didn't miss the warmth that filled his eyes when he met her gaze, or the flicker of bittersweet longing and remorse in his expression that matched the ache gripping her chest.

"No problem," he told Jon.

Her brother-in-law shoved to his feet and wiped his hands on his jeans. "When I stopped to check on our order today, the guy at the plumbing outlet said the shower unit should arrive by the end of the week."

"Good to hear." She stepped aside as Jon headed out of the bathroom and followed him downstairs, needing distance from Matt in order to collect her thoughts.

"Any chance you'll be finished with the shower this weekend?"

"With any luck." He gave her a measuring scrutiny. "You gonna be all right here alone with Randall if I go now?"

Randall. She sighed. "I see you talked to Robert."

He shrugged. "Robert said you took the news kinda hard. You holdin' up, okay?"

Her shoulders sagged. "I've been better, but I've also survived worse."

Jon scrubbed a hand over his jaw. "I knew the first time I saw him that he looked familiar. I recognized him from the newspaper pictures and TV coverage of his trial, but just couldn't place his face out of context."

"Jon, if this is going to be an I-told-you-so lecture, I'm really not in the mood."

He held up his hand. "No. No I-told-you-sos. But I don't understand why you didn't recognize him. Didn't the details of his case ring any bells for you?"

She folded her arms over her chest. "Why should they?"

Jon's eyes widened in disbelief. "Because it was Ryan's case!"

"Ryan and I never discussed his cases. You know that." She drew herself up and leveled her shoulders. "I didn't want to hear about the parade of murders and robberies and child neglect that he dealt with every day, and he didn't want to rehash his cases when we were together. That was our agreement from the beginning."

Ryan had wanted his home life unmarred by the seaminess he encountered at work, and the reminder of human nature's darker side, the details of the cases he prosecuted only depressed her.

"Ignorance is bliss?" The disapproval in Jon's tone chaffed, and she bristled.

"For me, it was. He knew I supported him and that was enough for us."

Jon pulled his keys from his pocket. "Well, maybe it's time you broke your rule and found out a little more about the case."

"Matt's already told me most of what happened, the evidence they had against him."

"He's given you his side. I mean get Ryan's take."

She tipped her head and gave Jon a curious look. "How?"

"Didn't Ryan keep a copy of his files here at the house somewhere?"

"Well, yeah. Sometimes he'd work from home on the weekend, so he kept a copy of all his case files in his office."

Jon turned up a palm. "So read Randall's file."

Holly scowled. "I can't—"

"Why not? Who'll know?" When she opened her mouth to protest, Jon stepped closer and placed a hand on each of her shoulders. "Robert told me his theories about Randall seeking you out for revenge. Now, I don't know if that's the case or not, but if I were you, I'd want to know all I could about what transpired in the courtroom between my spouse and Randall." He squeezed her shoulders before he stepped back. "Better safe than sorry, especially if you're gonna let Randall stay on until these renovations are finished."

Her stomach seesawed. She hated the idea of rifling through Ryan's files, invading his privacy. Or was it just that she was afraid of what she might learn about Matt?

Jon sent a meaningful glance up the stairs before he turned and headed out to his truck.

What if Jon was right? What if the answers she needed were downstairs, boxed up in her dusty basement?

Holly pressed a hand to her swirling stomach and shuffled into the kitchen to fix a cup of tea to soothe the riot in her gut. She took the kettle from the stove to the sink to fill it and was absorbed in her thoughts when the scrape of a chair startled her out of her musings. She spun around to find Matt watching her, one hand braced on the back of a chair.

"I think Jon's right," he said calmly.

"Excuse me?" She tipped her head in query.

"I think you should read Ryan's case brief. I want you to see that everything I told you is the truth."

Holly tensed. "You were eavesdropping?"

"Not intentionally. Jon's voice carries." He rocked back on his heels and set his jaw. Intensity and purpose blazed in his eyes. "I think you should look into Ryan's death, too. Read through the police files on that investigation."

Holly carried the kettle back to the stove and turned the burner on. "Matt, I don't—"

"You need answers, Holly. Closure. That's why you were in that old church the day we met. And now, with all these new questions and allegations against me, I want the opportunity to clear my name."

He moved closer, and the familiar scent of soap and spice teased her nose. Her traitorous body reacted to his proximity, her skin tingling and her senses hyperalert.

"You asked me earlier if I had something to do with Ryan's murder, and I welcome the opportunity to prove to you that I didn't." The conviction in his tone kicked up her pulse. "I'll work with you. We can go down to the police station together and talk to the investigating officer."

She stepped back, shaking her head, needing distance from him to think clearly. "I've already talked to Robert about—"

"Forget what Robert's told you. You told me that he always put you off when you questioned him in depth. He could easily have sugarcoated what little he told you or withheld information he thought would upset you. You need to get firsthand information, not some filtered, sanitized version from your over-protective brother-in-law."

She paced across her kitchen, debating, trying to sort out her tangled feelings. "You don't think Robert's been honest with me about the police investigation?"

He lifted a shoulder. "It's possible. I know that when you care about someone, sometimes it's hard to tell them news you know will cause them pain. If he did withhold information from you, I'm sure it was simply because he wanted to spare you unnecessary pain."

Matt's gaze locked with hers. The honesty and heartfelt emotion behind his argument held her spellbound, and the instincts that had told her to trust him from day one raised their voices again. The internal pull, the unique connection she felt with Matt battled with the ache of his deception, tying knots in her chest.

Do you really think he kept his connection to Ryan a secret out of malice? As Paige's question replayed in her head, tears filled Holly's eyes.

"All right. I want to know the truth. The whole truth. About everything. About you and Ryan and his murder."

When the kettle whistled, she jolted, then moved it from the hot burner with a sigh of resignation. "Before he left, Jon all but accused me of living in ignorance to protect my sensibilities. And in a lot of ways, he was right. But in doing so, all I did was open myself to more pain when the truth came home to roost. Well, no more." She faced Matt and gave a tight nod. "I'll pick you up at the Community Aid Center tomorrow afternoon. We'll start by talking to the police about Ryan's murder investigation."

The next afternoon, Holly tapped her foot nervously as she waited for the detective in charge of Ryan's case to meet with her and Matt. The lobby of the Morgan Hollow P.D. was not an especially busy place, but the ringing of phones and the clack of computer keys added to the buzz of adrenaline winding her tight.

Matt reached over from the next chair and placed a hand on her knee. Startled, she turned toward him.

"It'll be all right." His calm tone and steady gaze took the edge off her frayed nerves. Heat from his hand seeped through her slacks and spread a soothing warmth through her.

She huffed a sigh. "I don't know why I'm so jumpy."

"You don't know what you're going to learn. I can understand you being a little anxious." He sent her an unwavering look. "But whatever you find out, I'm here for you. Everything will be okay. You have to believe that."

Holly inhaled a slow, deep breath and gave Matt an appreciative grin. Her ragged pulse had almost returned to a normal rhythm, when a familiar voice called her name.

Robert strode toward her from the front door, a confused and concerned look darkening his face. He stripped off the overcoat he'd been wearing as he approached her and frowned when he noticed Matt beside her.

"What's happened? What are you doing here?" Robert draped his coat over his arm and braced a hand on his gun belt.

"Nothing's happened. I came to talk to Detective Parker about his investigation of Ryan's murder."

Robert stiffened his spine and squared his shoulders. "Why? Have there been new developments?"

Holly turned up a palm. "I don't know. That's why I'm here. I really know so little about the case, and it's time that changed."

Robert looked away for a moment and sighed before returning his gaze to Holly. "If you have questions about the case, you could've asked me. I've told you I'd keep you up-to-date."

She nodded. "I know. But secondhand information isn't enough for me anymore. I want to see the evidence, talk to Detective Parker myself. I want to know why the investigation has stalled out."

Robert's jaw tightened, and he slanted a dubious glare toward Matt. "I suppose he put you up to this."

"Yeah, I suggested it." Matt leaned back in his chair and draped an arm across the back of Holly's seat. His casual pose belied the tension she could feel radiating from him. "I knew she needed answers she wasn't getting from you. And I wanted to prove to her that I had nothing to do with Ryan's death. Despite your allegations."

"Mrs. Cole?" An older man in a suit coat and open-collared shirt addressed her from across the lobby.

Holly rose from her chair and gathered her purse, but as she turned to meet Detective Parker, Robert grabbed her arm. "Holly, are you sure you want to do this? I've tried to spare you the gory details, because I didn't want to tarnish your memories of Ryan."

Holly patted Robert's hand. "And I appreciate your looking out for me, but it's time I take off my blinders and learn the whole truth."

As she pulled free of Robert's grip, Matt placed a hand at the small of her back and escorted her to the small interrogation room with Detective Parker.

After introductions were made, Holly explained her frustration over being kept in the dark concerning the investigation and asked to see the detective's files.

Detective Parker rocked back in his seat and laced his fingers over his chest. "I'm sorry, Mrs. Cole. I was under the impression your brother-in-law was keeping you up-to-date."

"To an extent. But I want to see for myself the evidence that's been gathered."

The detective gave her a measured scrutiny. "You do understand that open case files are not open to the public. We have to keep our records confidential to avoid jeopardizing the case. If we tip our hand to the guilty party, they could use that information to cover their tracks. In fact, we're very selective about the information released to the press."

Holly flattened her hands on the conference table and leaned toward the detective. "But I'm the victim's wife. Aren't I allowed to know how the investigation is going?"

Detective Parker jerked a nod. "I'd be happy to keep you posted on my progress, but I still can't show you all my cards."

As Holly's frustration mounted, her muscles tightened.

Matt placed a wide hand on her shoulder and squeezed. "Could you tell us how the case stands now? Do you have any helpful leads, any suspects at all?"

Scooting his chair back, Detective Parker rose and adjusted his pants. "Tell you what…you wait here, and I'll go get the file on your husband's case. To be honest, I haven't looked at that case in several months. I'll tell you what I can, and try to answer any questions you have. Sound fair?"

Holly nodded. "Thank you."

When Detective Parker left the room, Matt wrapped his fingers around Holly's hand and stroked her wrist with his thumb. Rather than soothing her, his tender touch stirred a heady heat in her blood and evoked sensual memories of making love to Matt.

Making love. She'd chastised him for using that term, but she couldn't deny the emotion that had been behind her actions. Their nights together held a special place in her heart, and memories of their bodies intertwined created an achy longing to hold Matt again, to feel his hands on her skin.

She shifted in her chair to face Matt. "Doesn't sound like we'll get the information we'd hoped. Although…" She scoffed at herself. "What did I expect? I already knew they didn't have a suspect, that they had little evidence at all."

He smiled and brought her knuckles up to his lips for a soft kiss. "But you still hoped to find something that would ease your mind, give you a little peace."

"And maybe something that would clear you, as well."

She should've pulled her hand away, but somehow she couldn't. His gentle touch and the affection in his eyes held her spellbound.

He sent her a crooked grin. "Yeah, I'd kinda hoped for that, too."

The tender warmth in his expression speared Holly's heart, reminding her of the emotion that had filled his eyes as he'd joined their bodies. The affection and spiritual connection she'd experienced in his touch and seen on his face couldn't have been faked. Could it? Could her instincts about Matt really have been so far off base?

And even if she could believe he cared about her as he had claimed, how did she get past the secrets he had kept from her and learn to trust him again? Was that even what she wanted? She hadn't gone looking for a new relationship. Yet in the days since she'd evicted Matt from her house, she'd been lonelier than in the days following Ryan's death.

Holly nibbled on her bottom lip and sighed. Loneliness wasn't a good enough reason to let a man into her heart. She had to know there was a basis for a solid, trusting relationship and real love.

Matt brushed her hair back from her cheek and tipped his head to meet her eyes. "Holly? What's that sad look about?"

Before she could answer, the interrogation-room door opened, and Detective Parker strode back in. The file in his hand was disappointingly thin, and the consternation denting his brow stirred an uneasy prickle at the back of her neck.

He slapped the folder on the table and shoved his hands in his slacks pockets. "Here's what I have, but—" He scowled and stared at the file, flexing the muscles in his jaw.

"But?" Holly prompted.

"There are documents missing. Key reports, lab results, photos."

Matt shifted to the edge of his chair and leaned forward, narrowing a stunned look on the detective. "Missing? How is that possible?"

"I don't know. I lock my desk at night, and the file room has restricted access."

Holly shook her head, trying to make sense of this turn of events. "Could you have just misfiled the other documents? Or maybe someone borrowed the file to—"

"I know for a fact everything was still in this file the last time I reviewed it." He stabbed the file with his finger to emphasize his point. "Nothing was misfiled. And no one could have gotten the file without my knowledge."

"And yet key evidence is missing." Though calmly spoken, the challenge in Matt's tone was unmistakable.

Detective Parker straightened and glared at Matt. "Make no mistake, I will get to the bottom of this." He turned to Holly, adding, "I will find the person responsible for removing the documents and let you know when the evidence is recovered. I promise you, Mrs. Cole, I won't rest until I know who stole my file...and why."

Chapter 13

As they left the police station, Matt assessed Holly's pale face and trembling hands. News of the missing evidence had hit her hard. When she stabbed her key at the truck lock, he slipped the keys from her fingers and nudged her away from the door. "You're upset. Let me drive you home."

She only hesitated a second before nodding her assent. She slid across to the passenger seat and leaned her head back with a weary sigh. "They're never going to catch Ryan's killer, are they? These incompetent oafs can't even file key documents properly. They let evidence go missing, for crying out loud!"

Matt cranked the truck's engine, allowing Holly to vent her frustration. While Holly seemed inclined to believe the missing documents were the result of mismanagement and careless police work, Matt suspected something more nefarious was to blame. Ryan had been a high-profile prosecuting attorney. He could easily have made enemies in the community—even in the police department. Just because they were on the same side of law enforcement didn't mean his handling of cases sat well with all of his colleagues.

He glanced at Holly, whose drawn face and stunned expression told him she was in no frame of mind to hear his theories. She needed a soft, safe place to land as the weight of this latest trauma crashed down on her. If she'd let him, he intended to be that calm harbor for her.

She smacked the armrest with the flat of her hand. "I should have stayed closer to the investigation from the beginning and not let Robert spoon-feed me information like some fragile child who couldn't deal with the ugliness of her husband's murder." She heaved another shuddering sigh. "If I'd stayed in touch with Detective Parker, stayed on top of the progress of the case myself…" She clenched her teeth and growled.

He reached over to squeeze her shoulder. "Holly, don't beat yourself up over this. I think everyone wants to believe the police are infallible and that justice will always prevail. But the truth is, they're human. They make mistakes."

When she slanted a sharp look his way, he lifted a hand to forestall her argument.

"I'm not excusing sloppiness. Losing those documents is unconscionable. I'm saying you shouldn't blame yourself for expecting them to handle the case properly. It was a reasonable expectation."

"You know what my problem is?"

He angled a patient look toward her, allowing her to let off steam.

"I'm too trusting. I always have been. I always thought I had good instincts with people, always wanted to believe the best in people, give them the benefit of the doubt." She waved a hand as she ranted. "Ryan told me I was being naive, and I'd tell him he was just jaded because of his job. But maybe he was right."

Matt locked his attention on the winding mountain road as they left town and headed back to Holly's farmhouse. Guilt twisted inside him, knowing he was primarily responsible for her disillusionment. Holly's warmth and caring, her innocent belief in the goodness of humanity and her determination to show kindness to others were among the things he loved most about her. That he'd tarnished her simple faith and willingness to trust gouged a raw place inside him.

He'd hurt another woman he loved, and that was unforgivable. Holly would be better off if he walked away now and never looked back, his commitment to her renovations be damned.

But some misplaced protective inclination whispered to him to stay, to make sure she weathered this latest storm in her life. The healer in him wanted to mend her broken spirit and revive her zest for life. For the mistakes he'd made with Jill, for the hurt he'd caused Holly, he deserved to be alone. But Holly didn't. He wouldn't abandon her, wouldn't let her push him away until he knew she'd be all right.

Gripping the steering wheel, he searched for some way to comfort her and restore her hope. When they passed a house where a young boy played on a tire swing in the front yard, inspiration struck. "Hey, I almost forgot to tell you... I saw Missy Cramer and her daughter at the Center last night."

Holly turned a blank expression toward him. "Who?"

"The woman whose little girl had pneumonia. You bought her prescription for her?"

Her face brightened with recognition. "Oh, right."

"Her daughter's doing much better...thanks to you. Her mother asked me to tell you how grateful she was for your help."

Holly pulled her mouth into a half grin. "That's good to hear."

Matt drummed his thumbs on the steering wheel. "In fact, I've been thinking..."

He cast an expectant glance toward Holly. "I want to write up a grant request to start a free medical clinic at the Community Aid Center."

Holly blinked, and her gaze drifted away as she processed his idea. When her eyes found his again, the passion he'd hoped to tap lit her face.

"How would it work?" she asked, an excited energy underlying the question.

Matt's pulse kicked up. Maybe he couldn't change his past mistakes, but he could try to do some good to balance the scales. The thought of practicing medicine again invigorated him. For the first time since Jill's death, he wanted to return to pediatrics. Though he'd kept his medical license current and could have gone to another state, where his bad press didn't haunt him, to set up a new practice, he hadn't wanted to move that far away from his kids.

And, thanks to the depression he'd been in, he'd lost all interest in medicine—until recently. Helping Missy Cramer's daughter had prodded his dormant need to heal, to help.

He spent the rest of the drive to the farmhouse elaborating on his idea and logistics he'd hammered out as he'd painted her bathroom. Holly's enthusiasm for the project grew, evidenced by the vibrance of her expression and her voice as they made plans, and she offered a few viable options he hadn't considered.

She sat sideways on the truck seat, facing him when he parked in front of her house. "Have you ever written a grant request before? How long do you think it will take to put it together?"

"No, and I don't know. Guess it depends on how much time I can get on the computer at the library. I'll have to research funding, work up the action plan and put it all in a report."

She shook her head. "Use my computer. It's just sitting there all day. My Internet connection is slow, but it works."

He handed the keys back to her and narrowed a skeptical gaze. "Are you sure? You were pretty steamed Monday when you found me at your house working on renovations. Writing a grant request could take months."

Her face fell, and her shoulders slumped. "Oh, right." She rubbed her temple with her fingers and sent him a churlish frown. "Dammit, Matt! Why do you have to be so confusing!"

"Confusing?"

"I want to hate you for hurting me, for breaking my trust." Anger blazed in her eyes. "But then you go and have a brilliantly selfless idea to help homeless families, and have me believing you're kindhearted and generous and wonderful again."

He fought the grin that twitched on his lips. "Oh...sorry about that."

His attempt at levity fell flat, and when tears puddled in her eyes, his heart twisted. Matt scooted across the front seat and captured her face between his hands. He swiped the moisture from her cheeks with his thumbs and pressed a kiss to her forehead. "Holly, I will never forgive myself for hurting you. If you want me out of your life, I'll go. Say the word, and I'm gone. I just want to do what's best for you. I want to honor my commitment to finish the renovations, but if having me around is too painful, I'll leave and never bother you again."

Her eyes slid closed, releasing another fat tear from her lashes. "I want to trust you, but I can't. I want to forgive you, but I'm still hurt. I want to make love to you, but I'm scared."

"Scared?"

She nodded and opened her eyes. "Scared of falling in love with you. Scared of losing someone else I care about."

"Holly, I won't—" Matt caught himself and swallowed the words on his tongue. She'd left a wide opening for him to pledge his love and devotion.

And he'd almost promised her that he wouldn't leave her, that she had nothing to fear by loving him.

But how could he promise her anything? He had nothing to offer her. No home, no job, no family. When he'd had a wife, a home, a family, he'd made costly mistakes that had lost him everything. How did he know he wouldn't screw up again and let Holly down the way he'd failed Jill? He'd already broken her trust, shattered the fragile faith she'd put in him. Knowing his future was still murky and uncertain, he refused to give her any false expectations and risk doing further damage. The best gift he could give her was the ability to move on without regret.

She searched his gaze, waiting...

He sighed, his heart breaking. "I won't make promises I can't keep. I don't know what's down the road for me. But I cherish the time we've spent together. You will always hold a special place in my heart."

Her crestfallen expression spoke for her disappointment, and the pain that dimmed her eyes sliced him to the core.

"Well, then..." She wrenched free of his grasp and opened the passenger door. "It's good to know where we stand. You may use my truck to drive yourself home." She snatched her purse from the seat, clearly struggling to appear unscathed by his underwhelming response.

"Good night, Matt," she said.

But her tight tone, her wounded expression said goodbye.

The next morning, Holly carpooled to and from school with another teacher who lived on the outskirts of Morgan Hollow. By the time her colleague dropped her at home that afternoon, her Tacoma was parked in her driveway, and Matt was unloading a toolbox from the truck bed.

He smiled the warm greeting she'd come to miss since he'd moved out, and she shoved down the wistful longing his absence stirred. He'd been clear enough last night that he had no desire for a long-term relationship. She'd misread everything about their relationship from the start and made a fool of herself in the process.

She strolled over to the tailgate and indulged Matt in a stilted exchange about how her day had been.

"So...where do the renovations stand?" she asked, trying to sound casual and knowing she'd failed miserably. She might as well have asked, "How much longer will you be hanging around my house making me wish for something that will never happen, making me regret ever opening my heart to you?"

Matt gave her a knowing look, the kind of insightful gaze that had fooled her into believing they had some sort of spiritual connection, an unspoken understanding of each other's hopes and dreams.

"Maybe another week. I have a few little jobs to putter with until Jon gets here to install the shower." He lifted a bag from the truck bed. "After that I just have to lay the carpet in the hall upstairs and finish installing the light fixtures you picked out in the master bath and study." He flashed a lopsided grin. "Done by Christmas, like you wanted."

She tried to muster some pleasure at the thought of the work on the house finally being finished. But the end of renovations meant the end of her association with Matt, and the thought of never seeing him again hurt more than she cared to admit.

Holly huffed, frustrated with herself. Matt had deceived her and, last night, all but told her that he had no interest in working on a relationship with her. Even if she could move past her hurt over his withholding the truth from her about Ryan's connection to his case, the past few weeks had merely been a pleasant diversion for Matt until he moved on. A convenient affair with a lonely widow. An unexpected bonus to his renovation work.

The worst part was, she'd told herself all along to take it slow. She'd realized Matt had never made any promises of a lasting relationship, yet she'd dived in, anyway. She'd followed her heart rather than listening to her head, and now she was paying the price. She should be glad to be able to make a clean break from him and put her life back on track, but she couldn't deny that he'd left a mark on her heart. Putting him behind her and moving on would be difficult.

She headed inside and checked her answering machine,

hoping to have a message from Detective Parker that he'd located the missing portions of the file from Ryan's murder investigation. But her only call had been from Ryan's sister.

"I want to have a family birthday party for you on Christmas Eve," Jana chirped cheerfully. "We'll have dinner about 6:00 p.m., but if you want to come earlier, we can wrap Christmas presents together in the afternoon. Call me and let me know if that works for you."

Holly returned Jana's call and accepted the invitation. She thought about telling her sister-in-law what she'd learned concerning the evidence missing from the police file, but decided to give Detective Parker a few more days to track down the lost information before breaking the news to Jana.

When you care about someone, sometimes it's hard to tell them news you know will cause them pain. Matt's comment filtered through her mind, and her pulse stumbled. Was she guilty of the same crime she'd blamed Matt for? She shook her head. This was different. Wasn't it?

I think you should read Ryan's case brief. I want you to see that everything I told you is the truth.

The trip to the police station had sidetracked her yesterday from digging into the questions she had regarding Ryan's take on Matt's murder trial. But she had nothing planned for today and had nagging questions that needed to be addressed. She'd stored Ryan's files in the basement several months ago and not thought about them since. Now she couldn't stop thinking about them.

Jon hustled through the front door, yanking her from her thoughts. "Anybody home?"

She stepped around the corner from the kitchen and greeted Jon. "I'm here. And Matt's waiting upstairs. I hear y'all are going to install my shower today?"

Jon shucked off his blue jean jacket and hung it on the coat tree by the door. "Gonna try. I know you'll be glad to get back in your own bathroom."

"Amen to that."

He started for the stairs then paused. "Robert tells me that you and Randall were down at police headquarters yesterday, asking about Ryan's case."

Holly leaned against the door frame, crossing her arms over her chest. "We were."

"And? You learn anything new?"

She studied Jon's face for a moment, looking for what she couldn't say. "Not really. Turns out a good portion of the documentation of the crime scene is missing from the lead detective's file."

Jon turned, his expression shocked. "Say that again?"

"You heard me. You mean you didn't know?"

"Why would I know? Last time I talked to Parker about the case everything was there, sparse as it was."

"When was that?"

He frowned as he thought back. "Maybe September. He promised to call if they learned anything new, so I'd not bothered to check in recently." He pressed his mouth in a firm line. "Damn. How'd this happen? What did he say about recovering the lost information?"

"Just that he was determined to find it and he'd keep me posted."

"Do Jana and Robert know about this?"

"I haven't told them, but word could have gotten to Robert via the grapevine at the station."

Jon stared into near space scowling for a moment then, muttering a curse word, slapped the newel of the staircase handrail. As he started up the steps, Holly called to him. "If you need me, I'll be downstairs."

"What's downstairs?"

"Ryan's files. I'm taking your advice about learning his side of Matt's case. I'm done with living in ignorance. If I'd kept better tabs on what was happening with the investigation of Ryan's murder, maybe part of the file wouldn't be missing."

Jon shot her a frown of disagreement. "You have no control over what happens with police files."

Holly dismissed his reassurance with a shrug and detoured to the kitchen to start cooking dinner. She pulled a casserole she'd made several weeks ago from the freezer and slid it into the oven on low heat to bake.

Jon had only been upstairs a couple of minutes before she heard his footsteps on the stairs, and he poked his head around the corner from the front hall. "We've got the wrong size pipe fittings, so I'm going to make a quick run into town. Need anything?"

"No, thanks," she called as she finished washing the breakfast dishes, and he tromped out the front door. After starting a load of laundry, she decided she'd stalled long enough. The job ahead of her wouldn't get any easier because she'd procrastinated.

Opening the door to the basement, she peered down the stairs into the dank darkness. She'd not been in the storage space more than a couple of times since Ryan's death. The windowless rooms felt claustrophobic, and the boxes of Ryan's possessions were a heartbreaking reminder of her loss. Tugging the pull chain to click on the bare bulb that lit the steps, she started downstairs, shivering as a cold draft from the unheated basement whispered over her skin. At the bottom of the stairs, she shuffled into the large storage room to the left of the steps and jolted when the squeaky door slammed shut, sucked closed by the shifting air current as the furnace kicked on. After groping for the light switch, she found the large plastic storage boxes with the duplicate copies of Ryan's files but hesitated before opening the first snap-on lid.

Ryan's work had always been taboo, confidential and of no interest to Holly.

Now, she stared at the boxes of papers he'd meticulously kept as a backup to his office records and conjured an image of Pandora opening the box of evils and releasing chaos on the world. If Jon and Robert were right, if Matt was withholding ugly or incriminating truths about the case Ryan had against him, this box of Ryan's files could destroy the illusions she'd had about Matt. While she was angry about his deception, she still held to her belief that Matt was, at heart, a good man. A caring man. A man of integrity.

Yet Ryan had believed him guilty of murder. How could she reconcile that with what she knew about Matt?

Taking a deep breath for courage, she pried open the lid and lifted the first file, dated only a couple weeks before Ryan's death. Too recent to have been Matt's case. She set that file aside and moved on, digging deeper. She took out file after file, finding them chronologically stacked in reverse order, making it easy for her to sort through them and find the cases from the summer of Matt's trial. Finally she located a thick file marked "Randall murder."

Hands shaking, she lifted the file out and sat on the cold floor, cross-legged, perching the folder on her lap. After steeling her nerves, she cracked open the file. She scanned a few dry legal documents at the front, then paged forward, searching for Ryan's personal notes, documents regarding evidence or sworn testimony. When she flipped to graphic photographs from Jill's autopsy, Holly's lunch surged to her throat.

Squeezing her eyes shut, she shuffled blindly past the series of photos and swallowed the bile clogging her throat. Since Ryan's death, she'd had to face a lot of unpleasantness and grim realities from which her husband and parents had previously sheltered her. She drew on the core of strength she'd had to develop in recent months, knowing that she'd need all of her inner fortitude and conviction before everything settled, one way or another, with Matt. Glancing down at the file, heart trembling, she braved the next several pages, documents detailing Matt's arrest, the charges against him and transcripts of his answers when interrogated by the police.

A scuffing sound caught her attention, and she paused from her reading and glanced toward the storage-room door. "Hello? Matt, is that you?"

No answer.

"Hello? Who's there?" She listened carefully and heard nothing. Maybe she'd imagined the noise. The basement, with all its shadows and spiderwebs, made her jumpy. That was all.

Impatient with her needless jitters, she took a moment to relax her tense muscles before delving into the file again.

Holly read, absorbed by the materials in the file, until her back ached from sitting on the floor. Until a deep, weary breath called her attention to an odd odor.

She raised her head and sniffed the air again.

Smoke.

Her heart skipped nervously. What was burning? Had she left something on the stove?

Shoving to her feet, her muscles stiff from sitting so long on the concrete floor, Holly crossed the storage room. When she touched the doorknob, the metal burned her hand, and Holly gasped in shock.

The burning scent was far more pronounced by the door, and glancing down, she found black wisps of smoke curling through the crack at the base of it.

Her heart racing, Holly ran the back of her hand over the wooden door. Warm. Too warm. Evidence a fire burned just on the other side. Safety rules dictated she leave the door closed, keeping the fire and smoke at bay as long as possible.

But this was the only exit from the room. She had no choice but to open the door if she wanted to escape before the fire grew too large.

Adrenaline pounded through her, and she heard the blood swishing past her ears.

Pounding on the door, she shouted as loud as she could, "Help! Fire! Matt! Someone help me! Fire!"

The first fingers of hysteria closed around her throat.

No! Don't panic. Stay calm. Think.

Sucking in a calming breath, Holly stepped back from the door and wrapped her arms around her chest. She needed to call for help. 9-1-1. Of course.

She fumbled her cell phone out of her pocket and punched in the emergency number. As calmly as she could, she told the operator her address, about the fire and that she was trapped in the basement. But she knew, because of her remote location, it would take the fire trucks several minutes to reach her house.

She had to do something to save herself.

Could she crack the door open for a peek to see how far the fire had advanced? The storage room was quickly filling with black smoke. She coughed on the choking thick fumes, deciding the question for her. She didn't want to die here, not having tried at all to get out on her own.

Wrapping her shirt around her hand to protect her from the heated metal, Holly turned the knob and pushed.

The door didn't budge.

She shoved harder, her panic growing. Using all her strength, she managed to open the door an inch, enough to see someone had blocked the door with the large shelving unit from the opposite wall.

She *had* heard someone on the stairs. That *someone* had trapped her in the dark storage room.

And left her to die.

Chapter 14

Matt sat back on his heels and rolled the ache from his shoulders. He surveyed the shower unit in the middle of the bathroom floor and sighed. He'd done all he could with the installation until Jon returned from the hardware store.

As he did a bit of straightening from an earlier project, a thumping sound drifted through the heater vent. He stopped crumpling a plastic package wrapper long enough to listen. Was the furnace on the fritz? If so, that repair had to take priority tomorrow. Colder weather was settling into the mountains.

A muffled voice joined the distant sounding thumps. Holly's voice. He strained to listen.

Although he couldn't distinguish words, Holly's tone sent a tingle of alarm chasing down his spine. Something was wrong. She sounded scared, frantic.

Shoving to his feet, Matt jogged toward the stairs, ignoring the numb ache that set in from kneeling so long. "Holly?"

He charged downstairs, checking the living room, the front porch, the family room. As he neared the kitchen, he smelled the dark scent of toxic smoke. Not the fragrant scent of wood smoke from the fireplace or the telltale aroma of burning food, but the acrid, foul smoke of burning plastics and man-made fibers.

"Holly?" he shouted, real fear tripping through him now.

The kitchen was empty, but a haze of smoke filled the room. The smoke alarm sounded with a shrill screech that wound his nerves tighter. "Holly!"

Matt pulled his shirt over his nose, then grabbed a towel from the sideboard and dampened it quickly in the sink. Holding the wet towel over his nose and mouth, he scanned the room, searching for the source of the smoke. Black puffs rolled under the closed door to the basement. Had Holly noticed the fire and gone downstairs?

Matt's pulse drummed an anxious rhythm in his chest.

Grabbing the fire extinguisher from the pantry with one hand and holding the protective towel with his other, Matt rushed for the stairs. When he opened the basement door, he winced from the heat that slammed into him. Pulling the extinguisher pin, he hosed the flames dancing on the steps and waved futilely at the smoke clouding his vision. "Holly!"

Leading with a spray of foam from the fire extinguisher, he headed down the steps cautiously. Despite the towel over his mouth, Matt choked on the thick smoke. He almost turned back, desperate for a clean breath. But the notion that Holly could be lost somewhere in the toxic black clouds urged him forward.

Holly! his head screamed even though he could no longer draw enough breath to call out.

He stumbled blindly down the last steps. Using the fire extinguisher, he doused the base of the flames until the fire sputtered out. Sinking to his hands and knees, closer to the cleaner air near the floor, he felt his way through the smoke. He groped blindly for Holly, for the door he knew was at the other side of the small landing.

But instead of a door, he found a wooden structure. Shelves. During recent trips to the basement for tools or to bring up the Christmas decorations, Matt remembered seeing a shelving unit on the wall *opposite* the storage-room door.

Had he gotten turned around in the dense smoke?

He squinted through the haze, still groping with his hand, scooting forward on his belly. His hand bumped a large plastic container in his path, and he dragged it closer for a better look.

A gas can. Matt's gut tightened, but he had no time to consider all the ramifications of this find. He continued, feeling his way hand over hand, until he reached the far wall. The space where the shelves had been was empty.

He hadn't been disoriented. Someone had moved the shelf, blocking the storage-room door. But why?

An eerie prickling sensation chased down his spine.

"Holly!" he shouted, but smoke strangled his voice.

Behind him, the embers still sizzled. Thick smoke still clogged the air, smothering him. He had little time to find Holly and get out alive.

The need for clean air burned in his lungs, but he didn't dare take a deep breath. Pulling himself up to his knees, he shoved the emptied shelving unit out of the way and found a door knob.

With the towel over his mouth, he drew a shallow strangled breath, then used the protective cloth to turn the knob. Inside, he found Holly's limp body huddled on the floor. Bile surged into his throat.

Adrenaline and panic jolted him into action. Scrambling to his feet, he hoisted her into his arms and stumbled blindly toward the stairs.

When his lungs seized, deplete of oxygen, he took an instinctive breath.

Sour dense fumes clogged his throat, and he sputtered, coughed.

He had to get Holly out. Had to get to fresh air. Had to stay conscious…just long enough to…get her outside….

He staggered up the stairs, choking and gasping for air. In the kitchen, the smoke alarm still screamed, echoing the urgency pounding in Matt's brain.

He wouldn't, couldn't lose another woman he loved.

His heart jolted, twisted. He was falling in love with Holly. Despite all the reasons a future with her seemed impossible.

Somehow, acknowledging what Holly had come to mean to him gave Matt a second wind, the spurt of energy he needed to stagger with her through the mudroom.

He shouldered the screen door open. Falling to his knees and gulping cold December air, he laid Holly on the frozen ground. Once he'd drawn another cleansing breath or three, he stumbled back to his feet. Grasping Holly under her arms, he dragged her clear of the house and did a quick check of her vitals. She had a pulse, but he didn't detect signs of breathing.

He patted her cheeks, trying to revive her. "Come on, honey. Hold on. Breathe for me!"

When he got no response, his heart rose in his throat. Wasting no time, he dipped his head and started mouth-to-mouth resuscitation.

Matt's heart pounded an anxious rhythm as he blew one breath after another into Holly's lungs.

Finally she coughed, her head rolling to the side, and she sucked in a deep breath. Relief pierced the bubble of tension squeezing Matt's chest. He sat back on his heels and allowed her to cough again, allowed her to recover her own natural breathing rhythm, ragged though it was.

She blinked rapidly and lifted a panic-stricken glance. "Matt…" she rasped hoarsely.

"Shh, don't talk. Save your breath. You're okay now, sweetheart. You're safe."

In the distance, he heard the wail of sirens, growing louder, until the volunteer firefighters drove down Holly's driveway.

"It started in…the basement," he shouted to one of the

men between breaths, his voice gravelly and choked from inhaled smoke.

Firemen in their full bunker gear filed past him into Holly's house.

One of the firemen jogged toward him with a medical kit and dropped to his knees beside Holly. "What have we got here?"

"She was…in the basement…where the fire started," he gasped, his own throat raw and his lungs still clamoring for oxygen. "Don't know how long…she was breathing smoke."

Combined with the gas can and the unexplained fire, the moved shelf indicated foul play, but he'd keep that tidbit to himself until the police arrived.

As if conjured by his thoughts, a patrol car wheeled down Holly's driveway, kicking up gravel. Robert jumped from behind the wheel and raced over to Holly. Sending an accusatory glare toward Matt, Robert barked, "What happened?"

"Fire. Started in the basement."

Robert bit out an expletive and knelt beside Holly, who breathed oxygen through the mask the EMT held over her mouth and nose. "I was on my way home when I heard 9-1-1 dispatch all first responders to Old Pine Road. I had a hunch—" He glanced around at the fire trucks and huffed. "Looks like my suspicions were right."

"Robert—" Matt cleared his throat and met the police officer's gaze. "I found…a gas can downstairs."

Robert frowned. "You think this was arson?"

"Worse. Storage-room door…was blocked. Someone trapped Holly."

Hitching his thumbs in his gun belt, Robert sat back on his heels. His expression darkened. "What are you doing here anyway? I thought Holly kicked you out."

Matt tensed, not wanting to get into another confrontation with Holly's protective brother-in-law. "I was installing her new shower."

"I thought Jon was doing that."

Matt nodded. "He's helping."

Robert swept a glance around the yard. "So where is he now?"

"He had to…make a run to the hardware store."

Robert grunted and narrowed a suspicious gaze on Matt. "And where were you when the fire started?"

Matt balled his hands, furious with the insinuation that he'd tried to hurt Holly and heartsick at the notion of having to defend himself from criminal allegations again. "Upstairs. In the master bathroom. Waiting for Jon to get back."

When Holly clamped a hand on Robert's arm, he cut a side glance to her. With a brush of her hand, she knocked the oxygen mask away. "Matt…saved me. He got…me out."

Robert placed a hand over Holly's. "That doesn't mean he didn't start the fire, only that he had second thoughts about killing you."

Matt gritted his teeth, acid roiling inside him. "Why would I want to kill Holly?"

Robert sent him a hot glare. "Why did you kill your wife?"

"I didn't!"

"Stop!" Holly cried hoarsely.

An ambulance pulled into the driveway and parked beside Robert's patrol car. Another EMT hopped out and jogged over to assist Holly.

Pushed aside by the medical personnel, Robert shoved to his feet, his jaw rigid. "Holly, if Jon was at the hardware store, Randall was the only one here with you. Right?"

Matt stiffened. That bit of circumstantial evidence looked bad for him, but clearly someone else *had* been there. "Jon could've come back. Or a neighbor came by or—"

"Holly's nearest neighbor is miles from here," Robert interrupted. "And Jon has nothing to gain from killing her."

Matt rose to his feet and matched Robert's challenging stance. "Neither do I!"

"Oh, really?" Robert narrowed a menacing glare at him, and Matt bristled defensively. "Maybe you're worried about her digging into her husband's case against you, now that she knows who you really are."

Fighting to maintain his composure, to not rise to Robert's baiting, Matt leveled his shoulders and gritted his teeth. "You're wrong. I encouraged her to read the case files. I have nothing to hide."

"And yet you kept your real identity from her for weeks. What else are you hiding?"

"Robert!"

Holly's hoarse cry drew both men's attention. She struggled to her feet, wobbling and sucking air from the mask before sliding the apparatus aside to speak. "That's enough. If you find proof…that Matt has ever tried…to hurt me, I'll…listen. Until then—" She paused to inhale a deep breath of oxygen. "I've heard enough…accusations." She coughed and replaced the mask over her nose.

The paramedic placed a hand under Holly's elbow to steady her. "Ma'am, I think you should go with us to the hospital to get checked out."

She pointed at Matt. "He should, too. He—"

Another coughing fit seized her.

"Sir?" The EMT turned to him, and Matt accepted the medical attention the paramedic now focused on him. If nothing else, perhaps in the ambulance, on the way to the emergency room, he'd get a chance to talk to Holly.

He couldn't let her believe he had anything to do with setting the fire.

And they needed to figure out who *had* tried to kill her.

By the time she was released from the hospital late that night and Jana pushed her wheelchair out toward the parking lot, Holly could barely keep her eyes open. Knowing she wasn't seriously injured, Jon and Robert had stayed at the farmhouse, checking in with the arson team and police officers who would head up the criminal investigation. The fire damage had been limited to the basement and despite the stink of smoke, the farmhouse had been cleared for Holly's return. Jana, however, insisted Holly spend at least the first night with her and Robert in town, and Holly had relented. She hadn't been looking forward to being alone in the big country house, knowing someone had tried to kill her earlier today.

But why? Why would anyone want her dead?

"Holly?"

Snapping her gaze up at the sound of Matt's voice, his timbre a deep husky rasp thanks to the inhaled smoke, Holly started at the sight of him.

"I thought you were discharged hours ago," she said. Her throat still hurt, but her voice had returned to nearly normal.

"I was. But I waited. I wanted to talk to you."

Holly angled her head to see Jana. "I know it's late, but would you mind giving me a few minutes?"

Jana returned a worried look. "Are you sure you feel up to it?" Then to Matt, "Couldn't this wait? It's been a long day for everyone."

"Just five minutes. Please." His gaze beseeched her, and Holly nodded.

After Jana stepped aside, Matt crouched in front of the wheelchair and reached for Holly's cheek. "What did your doctor say? Are you all right?"

Robert's accusations rang in her ears, and she warily pulled away from his touch, even though a secret part of her longed to throw herself into his arms and hide in the solace she'd once found in his embrace. "I'll be fine. I'll sit out from school for a day or two and rest, just to be sure though."

"Good." He exhaled deeply as if he'd been holding his breath, worrying about her, a sentiment mirrored in the tiny lines etched beside his eyes.

The notion that Matt had been concerned about her burrowed into her with a bittersweet pang.

"And you?" she asked.

A corner of his mouth twitched. "I'll live." He sobered and leaned closer, pitching his voice softer. "Holly, there's a lot about the fire today that bothers me. Not the least of which being the evidence that someone purposely trapped you in the basement."

Holly curled her fingers into her palms. "It just doesn't make any sense. Are you sure the shelf was moved, that it didn't just fall over?"

"I'm positive. And there was a gas can sitting on the floor, plain as day. As if whoever did it wanted the police to know it was arson." Matt pressed his mouth in a thin line, and Holly's fingers itched to stroke the lips that had teased hers with sultry kisses and lifted her spirits with warm smiles.

Swallowing hard to force down the emotions that climbed her throat, Holly met Matt's gaze. "Why would they be so blatant? To scare me?"

He scrubbed a hand over his already mussed hair and frowned. "I don't know, Holly. But I'm worried about you. We need to figure out who's doing this and why. What were you doing downstairs, anyway?"

"That's where I'd stored Ryan's old case files."

He raised his chin, and his jaw tightened. "So you *were* researching my case."

A statement, not a question.

She arched an eyebrow. "Does that bother you?"

"Why should it? I've told you, I told Robert, I'll tell anyone who asks—I have nothing to hide. I didn't kill my wife. I didn't kill Ryan." He cupped her cheek with his palm and drilled her with a penetrating gaze. "And I didn't try to kill you today. I lo—" He stopped abruptly, his breath catching.

Holly squeezed the armrests of the wheelchair, her heart thundering against her rib cage.

Matt closed his eyes and exhaled before lifting searching, vulnerable eyes to hers. "I love you, Holly. I don't know where we're supposed to go from here. I still have nothing to offer you, but…the last thing I want is to hurt you. Physically or emotionally. Please believe that."

Jana's footsteps signaled her approach, but Matt's gaze never wavered. Believing Matt, losing her heart to him would be so easy. But she'd been taken in by his charm and apparent sincerity before, and he'd deceived her. The attempt on her life today changed everything. Until she knew who'd started the fire, how could she risk trusting anyone?

What if Robert was right about Matt? Matt *had* been the only one at the farmhouse with her.

"Ready to go?" Jana asked, hanging a step back.

She held up a finger, asking Jana for one more minute, then met Matt's expectant gaze. Her heart rose to her throat, nearly strangling her words. "I need time to sort things out. Please don't come around the house anymore. I'll have Jon finish the renovations." She paused when her voice cracked. "Goodbye, Matt."

Chapter 15

In the weeks leading up to Christmas, Jon eventually finished Holly's renovations on his days off from the fire department, before turning his attention to repairing damage caused by the fire. The preliminary report from the fire marshal confirmed the fire had been an act of arson, and the police reported that the only fingerprints recovered from the gas can belonged to Matt. Holly heard through Robert that Matt had been brought in for questioning, but he'd staunchly denied responsibility for the fire. The fingerprints alone hadn't been enough to arrest Matt, but Robert made no secret of his suspicion of Matt. Holly found it hard to believe Matt had tried to kill her, but, as Robert pointed out, no one else had the opportunity or motive.

Detective Parker still had no leads on the missing evidence, and Holly was no closer to figuring out who or what to believe about any of the past months' events. She dragged through the motions teaching her class until they were dismissed for Christmas break, then huddled in her living room like a hermit, replaying her memories of time spent with Matt. Every couple of days, she called Paige for updates on the search for Zoey, but no one had heard from her.

A series of snowstorms hit Morgan Hollow just before Christmas, blanketing the mountains with a thick layer of snow and ice and giving her an excuse to hide out at home when Jana or Kim called asking her to have lunch.

Finally, after a few days of moping and procrastinating, she retrieved the boxes of Ryan's files, salvaged from the basement and only slightly smoke-and water-damaged, and buried herself in Matt's case.

As Matt had suggested, she found little in Ryan's file that contradicted Matt's version of what had happened the night Jill died. Ryan's case, it seemed, had been based largely on Matt's "confession" the night of Jill's death and other circumstantial, though highly incriminating, evidence. Ryan had focused on Matt's fingerprints on the gun, the condition of the upended room that suggested a struggle, and testimony of family friends that detailed the problems Matt and Jill had had in their marriage.

One afternoon, her third straight day of reading legal briefs and tedious testimony, she found a handwritten note Ryan had exchanged—perhaps in court?—with a colleague. Ryan had not been able to explain why no gunshot residue had been found on Matt's hands, but, to her dismay, Ryan had glossed over that inconsistency at the trial.

"Ryan, how could you?" Acid and disillusionment roiled in her gut. "You ignored key evidence? What happened to upholding the law?"

She couldn't discount that evidence of Matt's innocence so easily. While it disturbed her to think of Ryan railroading a conviction against Matt to advance his career, she found printouts of e-mails from Ryan's boss, pressuring him to win the high-profile case at all cost.

She glanced across the room to the portrait of her and Ryan that was on the mantel, and she addressed his image. "Is that

why you went after Matt so aggressively? To save your job?"
She sighed and shook her head. "That doesn't excuse anything.
You were dealing with a man's life, his future, his reputation!
Didn't that count for anything?"

*But the jury still found him not guilty. They believed him and
his lawyers over me. I didn't win,* she imagined Ryan contend-
ing.

"That doesn't change the facts of what you did. That trial
and the repercussions ruined his life!"

The house phone rang, jarring her out of her one-sided
argument with Ryan.

She picked up the cordless receiver and checked the caller
ID before answering. The display only read, "out of area." She
considered ignoring the call, but on the off chance it was Detective Parker with news about the missing documents for
Ryan's case, she punched the talk button.

"Happy early birthday, sis!" Zoey's lilting voice sang.

"Zoey!" Holly clenched the phone tighter, as if she could bring
her sister closer by squeezing the receiver with all her might.
"Thank God! Where are you? We've all been worried sick!"

Zoey gave a dramatic groan. "I'm fine. I'm with Derek, and
I'm safe."

"Define *with Derek.* Where is that on a map?"

"If I tell you, you'll just tell Dad, and he'll try to force me
to come home and…well, I can't do that."

"Why not? Zoey, Dad is a reasonable guy." Zoey interrupted Holly with a snort of disagreement, but Holly continued, undaunted. "If you'd just sit down with him and talk your
differences out. Heck, I don't even know what your fight was
about, but it couldn't be worth giving up your family and
hiding out God knows where."

"You can say that, because Dad never tried to bribe your boyfriend into leaving you." Bitterness dripped from Zoey's tone.

"He did what? No, Zoey, you must have misunderstood!
Dad would never—"

"Throw his wealth and power around to get his way? Holly, that's *all* Dad does. That's how he built Bancroft Industries. But I won't let him dictate my life the way he's dictating Paige's."

Knowing her sister's tendency toward hyperbole, Holly ignored most of Zoey's histrionics. But her comment about Paige niggled. Holly had picked up on a general discontent when she'd spoken to Paige and wondered if Zoey had any insight. "How is he dictating Paige's life?"

"Hello! She doesn't love Brent! She's marrying him because Dad wants her to, because it's good for Bancroft Industries. Brent is Dad's heir apparent as CEO when he retires next year, and he wants control of the company to stay in the family."

"But Paige has never told me—"

"Of course she hasn't said anything, even to you. She's doing her martyr-for-the-family act again. The good girl doing exactly as she's required. Well, it was killing me to see her throw her happiness away with that stuffed shirt. If she wants to do Dad's bidding, she can, but I want no part of it. And I especially didn't want Dad meddling in my love life."

"So…what happened with Derek?"

Zoey harrumphed. "Dad hated the fact that Derek didn't have a steady income or a white-collar job."

"What does Derek do?" Holly held her breath. There was no telling what kind of guy Zoey had gotten involved with.

"He's a professional poker player, and he's very good. His winnings are enough for us to live off of…most of the time."

"And the rest of the time?"

"My savings get us through for now."

Holly's heart sank. No wonder her dad was upset. Zoey's situation reeked of a shyster using her sister to support a gambling addiction.

"I'd get a job, too," Zoey was saying, "but we're on the road too much, traveling from one tournament to the next, so it isn't practical."

Holly bit her tongue to keep from saying something she knew would upset her sister. Zoey wasn't communicating with the rest of the family, and Holly didn't want to do anything to cut off the line of communication she had with Zoey—one-sided though it was. "Promise me something, will you? Stay in touch with me from now on. No more communication black-outs like the past few weeks. You really had us worried."

Zoey mumbled something Holly took as assent, then chirped, "Enough about me. How's that hunky roommate of yours? If I know you, you're planning a big Christmas together. Am I right?"

The mention of Matt lodged a sharp shard of pain in her heart. "Actually, no. Matt moved out. I'm supposed to spend Christmas with Jon, Jana and Robert."

"Whoa, back up. Why did Matt move out?"

Holly considered brushing the question off, but before she knew it, she was spilling the whole sordid story to her sister. When she finished, Zoey was unusually quiet. "Hey, are you still there?"

"Mmm, yeah, I'm just wondering what the problem is. You're incredibly attracted to this guy, he made you happier than you've been in more than a year, your instincts tell you he's a good person, a man of character and intellect and com-passion, but you kicked him out of your house? I don't get it."

Holly grunted her exasperation. "How am I supposed to trust him again? He lied to me!"

"Because he didn't want to hurt you! In fact, from what you just said, he was painfully honest about some rather intimate and difficult parts of his life—including giving you the truth about his connection to Ryan when you asked him about it. Can't you give him credit for that? Given all you know about him and the difficult position he was in, can't you understand what he did and why?"

Holly shook her head, knowing Zoey couldn't see her action, then argued, "Even if I could, how do I know he'll not betray me in the future? How do I know all the things Robert suspects about Matt aren't right? What if he did seek me out for revenge against Ryan? What if he did try to kill me in the fire? What if he—"

"Oh, give me a break! You don't really give any of Robert's theories credence, do you?"

"He's a cop. Why shouldn't I trust his instincts?"

"He may be a cop, but, remember, I've met the guy. He always struck me as a selfish, arrogant blowhard."

"Zoey!"

"Sorry, Hol. I know he's Ryan's brother-in-law, but I never liked the jerk."

"Even if he's a bit much at times, I know he has my best interests at heart. If he doesn't trust Matt, maybe he has good reason."

"And maybe you have a better reason *to* trust him. You know Matt. You know his heart. You've always had spot-on instincts about people, and you knew from the start Matt was trustworthy. You would never have hired him or let him move into your home if you hadn't been sure, deep in your soul."

Holly rubbed her temple and sighed. "But I—"

"Don't doubt your instincts now, Holly." Passion filled her sister's voice. "Don't doubt what you've seen to be true about him in the weeks you've spent together. He made a mistake but for all the right reasons. You have to forgive him and give your relationship another chance! Don't throw away your shot at happiness because he couldn't bring himself to broach a touchy subject as soon as he should have."

Holly sagged back on the sofa. Leave it to Zoey to appeal to the bottom-line emotional issue. The crux of the issue wasn't that Matt had keep an explosive secret from her. The real question she faced now was could she forgive him? Could she justify losing him from her life over his mistake, when in every other area he'd proven trustworthy?

"That still doesn't settle the question of who started the fire and why. He has to be the lead suspect, because his fingerprints were on the gas can. He was the only one here with me."

"That you know of. Someone could have been hiding in the barn. Or come and then left again. Or…who knows! Don't convict him on circumstantial evidence."

Holly's thoughts jumped to the files she'd been reading regarding Jill's death. So much of what Ryan had tried Matt on had been circumstantial. But she believed in his innocence in Jill's death, didn't she?

"I'll think about what you've said, Zoey, but…I'm scared."

"Of what?"

"Being wrong about him and being hurt again. On the other hand, I'm scared of losing him, too. I could love him." She plucked at the loose thread on her sofa, and her admission arrowed to a vulnerable place in her soul. She sighed her resignation. "It would be so easy to give him my heart."

"So do it! Follow your heart! Don't analyze this to death like Paige would."

She gave her sister an ironic laugh. "There is a balance, you know, between Paige's overthinking and your impulsiveness."

"Ahem, I prefer to think of it as my spontaneity and zest for life," Zoey said with a theatrical expansiveness.

"And I love your zest for life, squirt." Using her sister's childhood moniker brought a lump to her throat. "Don't ever change."

"Never. I promise. Look, I gotta go. Have a happy birthday tomorrow and remember I love you."

"You, too. Stay in touch. Or at least answer your cell when I call from now on."

"I will. But don't worry about me. I'm okay. I'm happy."

Holly disconnected the call and sat in her living room, staring into the fireplace as evening darkness gathered outside. Zoey's optimism and encouragement served as a counterbalance to Robert's voice of gloom and doom regarding Matt.

Don't throw away your shot at happiness.

Was that what she'd be doing if she didn't give Matt another chance?

Or was Matt the consummate actor, deceiving her on all

levels? Could he really be responsible for killing Ryan? Was she the next target in his plot for revenge?

Christmas Eve morning, the overcast skies and light snow matched Holly's mood following her restless night's sleep.

"Happy birthday," she told her reflection glumly in her freshly renovated bathroom. The completion of the project should have buoyed her spirits, but without the two men she most wanted to share the pride of completion with, Ryan and Matt, she could muster little enthusiasm. Before she dressed for the day, she did find some pleasure in the hot bubble bath she took in the claw-foot tub. The warm water and scented soaps soothed her tense muscles and helped calm the whirlwind of thoughts replaying fruitlessly in her head.

Her parents called to wish her a happy birthday, and she had to work to hide the emotion in her voice. She didn't want to upset her folks when there was nothing they could do to resolve the uncertainty she faced about Matt, about Ryan's unsolved murder, about the arson in her basement. She told her family about her talk with Zoey, reassuring them she was safe. She swore up and down she hadn't learned anything about her sister's whereabouts other than that she moved from town to town too much with Derek to get a job.

Paige was next to call and the conversation was much the same. Except that Paige reiterated her decision to postpone her wedding until Zoey came home. If Paige was upset by the decision to delay the nuptials, Holly didn't hear it in her voice, lending credence to Zoey's theory that Paige didn't really love Brent. In fact, Holly would swear Paige sounded relieved to have more time before her wedding.

Holly blew her bangs out of her face with a puff. Like she needed something else to worry about! Zoey and the possible swindler. Paige's reasons for marrying. Ryan's murder. The fire. Matt's lies….

Holly made herself a piece of toast and some coffee and

went to the bay window of her kitchen to watch the snow falling. Any other year, she'd be thrilled to be having a white Christmas. She still loved to build snowmen and make snow angels and have snowball fights, but without anyone to share it with, the snow was simply…lonely. Lovely but lonely.

She pictured the kids from her class playing in the snow with their friends and mustered a smile of appreciation for their sake. When she finished her breakfast, she bundled into her coat and boots to head out to the barn with fresh food and water for Magic and her kittens.

The kittens were balls of furry energy now that loved to play in the shelter of the barn but would scamper back to their bed, mewling for their mother, if they strayed too far from home base. This morning, the kittens were huddled close to each other and their mother, bracing against the icy drafts that seeped through the barn walls.

Holly took one look at the cold kitties and her heart melted. "Okay, if you promise to behave, you may come inside."

Magic watched warily as Holly scooped the wiggly kittens in her arms and clicked her tongue for Magic to follow her inside. Magic trotted behind her, following her babies' mewls.

Inside, Holly set the kittens up in a corner of the kitchen with a litter box, towels for a bed and plenty of food and water. She shut the kitchen door to keep the cats contained. As she passed through the entry hall on her way upstairs to change clothes before going over to Jana's for gift wrapping and her birthday dinner, she heard the scuff of feet on her front porch.

Through the door's window, she saw a shadowy figure. Even without opening her door, she recognized the height and broad-shouldered build of the man outside.

Matt.

Her breath hung suspended in her lungs while conflicting emotions battled inside her. Pleasure and anticipation of seeing him warred with the lingering anger, hurt and suspicion. When he knocked, she moved stiffly to open the door.

Wearing only a thin jacket, Matt stood with his shoulders hunched against the cold. His cheeks were ruddy from the icy temperature, but his blue eyes held the ever-present warmth that never failed to trigger a soul-deep answering heat within her.

"Hi." His eyes searched hers tentatively, measuring her mood. "Is this a bad time?"

"Not really. But I have to leave soon to go to Jana and Robert's."

He nodded. "Oh. Well, I won't keep you."

She scanned the front lawn, saw tire tracks in the snow but no vehicle. "How did you get here?"

He held up his thumb. "Hitched. Young guy home from college gave me a lift." He dug in his jacket pocket and pulled out a small box tied with a blue ribbon. "I just wanted to give you this." He extended the tiny package to her. "Happy birthday."

Holly's heart kicked, largely because of the effort he'd gone to in order to bring the present. "You remembered."

His cheek twitched in a grin. "It's a pretty easy birthday to remember considering it comes the day before a major Christian holiday."

She looked at his offering and hesitated. "Matt, you didn't have to get me anything."

"Don't start that. Just take it."

Holly opened Matt's gift with trembling fingers. The ribbon fell away, and she lifted the lid of the small box. Inside, nestled in tissue paper, lay a small wooden bird with outstretched wings. A metal loop was affixed to the bird's back so that it could be suspended.

She stared at it, speechless for a moment, until Matt reached for the wrappings. She handed the box to him so she could more closely examine the figurine.

"It's beautiful. It looks like—"

"The dove in your stained glass," he said at the same time she said, "the bird in my stained glass."

She lifted a corner of her mouth. "So the resemblance is intentional."

"Absolutely. It's an ornament for your tree. I made it from the piece of the trunk we cut off when we put your tree in the stand."

Holly sniffed the bird, savoring the pine scent of the smoothly sanded wood.

"I hope it, like the window, will remind you that you have an inner strength that will pull you through anything." Matt's voice dipped low and reverberated through her. "You can survive even the darkest times if you have faith and hope, and you'll find your wings again."

Her breath caught, and emotion clogged her throat. For several seconds, she could only stare at Matt through tear-puddled eyes. "And you?"

He seemed startled by her question. "What about me?"

"You've been through some pretty bleak times in recent years. Do you still believe you'll recover, that you'll find your way back?"

He ducked his head, furrowing his brow, before raising a penetrating gaze. "I've decided I don't want my old life back. Except for my children, I want no part of my past anymore."

A particularly stout, cold wind buffeted them, and she drew him inside by the arm and closed the door. "What are you saying? That you're giving up? Matt, you can't—"

"No. I'm not giving up, just shifting my focus. My priorities are different."

Holly squeezed the small bird figurine until the metal loop bit into her palm. "What are your priorities now? What do you want?"

He stroked a cold hand along her cheek, and she shivered, more from his gentleness and the longing he stirred in her than his icy fingers. "I want you, Holly, and I'm willing to fight for you. I'm willing to do whatever it takes to prove my innocence to you and earn back your trust."

She stepped back, away from his caress, and closed her eyes. She couldn't think straight when he touched her, and she needed all her faculties to decide how to respond.

"What about your kids? Your medical career?"

"I still want my kids, of course. I won't give up on getting them back." He rolled his shoulders and rubbed the cold from his hands. "And there are better ways I can employ my medical skills than private practice. I'm going to write that grant request I mentioned to include positions for a skeletal staff."

"With you as the lead doctor?"

He shrugged. "That'll be up to the executive board at the Community Aid Center. But yeah, I'd apply."

A smile, born of the warmth his selflessness and caring fired inside her, spread across her face. "They'd be crazy not to hire you."

He flashed a quick grin, then grew pensive. "Holly, I love you. I—"

She raised a hand and took another step back.

"I need more time. I'm still…confused. I have to be sure before…" Hugging herself, she rubbed the chill that chased up her arms.

He jammed his hands in his pockets and nodded. "Take all the time you need. I want you to be sure, too. I don't want you to have any doubts about who I really am, what I stand for, or how much I care about you."

Her shoulders sagged. "Believe me, nobody's more ready to put all this behind me than I am. It's just with Robert telling me one thing, raising all these questions about everything from Ryan's case to the fire, and Zoey encouraging me to follow my heart…my head has been spinning the past few days. I trust Robert, but I also trust Zoey. And I want to trust you. But how do I reconcile all the different advice and opinions?"

"I kind of like what Zoey told you. Trust your heart. And—" Matt snapped his mouth closed abruptly and sighed.

"And what?"

He shifted his weight and angled a reluctant glance toward her. "Well…I've been thinking a lot about Robert's accusations, his hostility toward me, and it got me wondering."

When he paused, she prodded, "Go on."

"Did he play any role in the investigation when Ryan was killed?"

Holly stiffened, wary where his line of questions was going. "No. He couldn't. It would've been a conflict of interest. But…he was one of the first ones on the scene when Ryan was found. I think he was *the* first one on the scene."

"Why was that?"

"He told me…" Holly braced a hand on the banister to the stairs and dug up old memories. "He and Ryan had arranged to meet at the old church so Robert could help with…something, but when Robert got to the church, Ryan was dead." Holly lifted her gaze to the stained glass over her door. "Robert thinks Ryan may have wanted to salvage that window, the same as I wanted to when I saw it."

Matt shrugged. "I suppose it's possible." He paused, and his gaze darkened. "Holly, if Robert was the first person on the scene after Ryan was killed, he had the opportunity to alter the scene or destroy evidence."

"Why would he do that? He's a cop! He knows crime scene procedures. He wouldn't do anything to tamper with evidence!"

"Are you sure about that? What if he's covering for somebody?"

Holly bristled. "What are you saying?"

Matt raised both hands, palms out. "Just think about it, Holly. As a cop, he's at the police station every day. He has access to the evidence room. He could have even gotten to Parker's file."

"You think Robert messed with the investigation? That he tampered with evidence?"

Matt pressed his lips in a firm line. "I don't really know.

I'm just trying to look at this thing from all angles. I wouldn't want to convict Robert on circumstantial evidence—even though that's how he's trying to incriminate me. But think about this—Robert was also one of the first people on the scene here after the fire. He says he was on his way home, but what if he came here, set the fire, then went down the road a little ways to wait for the fire trucks to arrive?"

Holly nearly choked. "Are you out of your mind? What possible motive could he have?"

"What motive does Jon have? What motive do I have?" Frustration vibrated in his voice. "I know it's a long shot, but it makes as much sense as anything else." He squared his shoulders. "In fact, if you go with the theory that he tampered with evidence in Ryan's case, maybe he does have a motive. Maybe he was trying to kill you to keep you from finding out that he interfered with a police investigation. Or maybe he was just trying to scare you. Maybe he was trying to frame me. Hell, Holly, I don't know!" Matt's tone grew uncharacteristically loud, and a blaze of conviction lit his eyes. "But the more I look at Robert's role in all of this, the more questions I have."

Lifting a trembling hand to her mouth, Holly drew a ragged breath. "He's family. Jana's husband. Ryan's brother-in-law. He wouldn't —"

But she couldn't finish the thought. How did she really know what Robert would or wouldn't do if pushed in a corner?

Matt stood with his arms akimbo and his head down. He heaved a deep sigh and raised weary eyes to her. "I'm sorry, Holly. I didn't mean to upset you like this on your birthday. I never should've brought this up now. But if you're going to be making a decision about our future, about who to believe, I think you need all the facts."

She raised her chin a notch. "Or maybe you're just trying to throw suspicion off yourself."

His jaw tightened, and a muscle jumped in his cheek.

Profound sadness filled his eyes, and he shook his head. Silently, he turned and headed for the door.

"Matt, wait!"

He stopped with his hand on the doorknob but didn't turn.

"Don't go. I just— You've given me a lot to think about and—" Holly sank down on the bottom step of the staircase. Raking her hair back from her face with her fingers, she tried to wrap her brain around all the twists and possibilities Matt had suggested. None of the events of the past few weeks, the past several months since Ryan's death made any sense to her. How could she follow her heart when her heart didn't know what to believe, who to believe, how to feel?

"I have to go to Jana and Robert's now. They're having a family birthday party for me and—" She stared at Matt, her heart thundering against her ribs. "Wait here for me. I shouldn't be too late. I want to talk. I want—" *To hold you, to make love to you, to go back to how things were between us before reality and doubt crashed down on us.*

He held her gaze, an unspoken connection and longing as evident in his eyes as she knew it was in hers. "Holly, I—" A loud thump from the kitchen interrupted whatever he meant to say. He jerked his gaze toward the closed kitchen door. "You have company?"

She pushed to her feet, shaking her head. "No, I brought the kittens inside from the cold. Lord only knows what mischief they're up to." She tipped her head toward the next room. "Perhaps you could check on them, keep them from destroying the house while I'm out?"

He agreed with a nod and an easy grin. "I'll wait for you."

Chapter 16

Holly stomped snow off her boots on Jana's front porch as she waited for someone to answer her knock.

When her sister-in-law opened the door, she pulled Holly into a warm hug. "There's the birthday girl! Come on in and get warmed up. Robert made a fire in the living room, and I've got a pot of coffee brewing."

Holly hung her coat on the rack in the entry hall and followed Jana to the living room. Savory scents of homemade bread and roasting beef filled the air. "Dinner smells wonderful as always. Thanks for doing this."

"My pleasure." Jana smiled warmly.

"How were the roads? Any trouble getting here?" Robert stood from his lounge chair and greeted Holly with a chaste kiss on the cheek. The scent of alcohol clung to him, and she sighed mentally. She prayed Robert's drinking wouldn't become a factor to spoil the evening as it had on Thanksgiving.

"A few icy spots. You have to be careful, but the roads are still negotiable for now."

Robert gave her a firm look. "Well, if it gets dicey, you're staying here tonight. No arguments. I think Santa will still find you." He added a wink as he headed back to his chair.

"Thanks, but I plan to head home before it can get treacherous. I—" She hesitated. "I have someone waiting for me at home."

Robert stiffened, and Jana tipped her head inquisitively. "Who?"

She divided a reluctant gaze between them. "Matt. He brought me a birthday gift, and...well, we have a lot to talk over."

Robert grunted in disgust. "Holly, what's wrong with you? Why can't you see that he's using you?"

Jana sent her husband a warning look. "Not today, Robert."

Robert tensed, but he inhaled a deep breath and nodded to his wife.

Jana twitched an awkward smile to Holly. "Jon and Kim are running late, but they'll be here in a while. I'll be back in a minute. Make yourself comfortable."

Holly gave Robert a wary glance as she moved closer to the fireplace and warmed her hands. The questions Matt had raised about Robert's involvement in Ryan's investigation, in the fire at her house, paraded through her head. She couldn't shake the uneasy feeling that she was missing something obvious. Playing nice with Ryan's brother-in-law, who was unpredictable at best when he was drinking, would be hard enough tonight without the doubts that plagued her.

"Here you go."

Holly jumped when Jana spoke, jarring her from her thoughts. She turned to accept the steaming mug of coffee Jana offered. "Thanks."

Jana helped carry the conversation by asking about Holly's family, her kindergarten class and her completed renovations. "I'll have to stop by and see the finished product. I'm sure it's beautiful."

Jon and Kim arrived, and dinner was served along with

birthday cake and more coffee. Holly had to force herself to eat. Watching Robert drink scotch throughout the meal did little to calm her jitters.

Her thoughts kept drifting to Matt, waiting for her at home, and to the suspicions he'd raised about Robert. By the end of the evening, after they'd said goodbye to Jon and Kim, Holly couldn't bite her tongue any longer.

"Robert," she said calmly when she had a moment alone with him while Jana excused herself to the bathroom. "Before he died, Ryan mentioned to me that he was concerned about your drinking. And I have to say, recently it has bothered me, too."

He tensed visibly. "I don't have a probl'm, if that's what you're sayin'."

"It's just that I've noticed you've been drinking a lot, and—"

"Ya know," he interrupted, aiming a finger at her belligerently, "if your husband had minded his own bus'ness, none of this would have happened."

An icy tingle nipped her neck. "None of *what* would have happened?"

A look of horror flashed over Robert's face, and he shook his head hard. "Nothing. I— Never mind."

"None of what would have happened?" Holly repeated emphatically.

Robert glared at her. "Drop it."

Suspicion tickled her spine, and dread turned the food in her stomach to rocks. "Robert, do you have access to Detective Parker's file concerning Ryan's murder?"

Color suffused his face. "That's not my case. I've told you everything I know, everything Parker's told me."

Holly squared her shoulders and plowed on. "That's not what I asked. Could you get access to Detective Parker's files?"

"You think I took the missing evidence, don't you?" Robert clenched his fists and his jaw defensively.

Holly hesitated. "I'm not saying that. But I'm trying to fill in some blanks, and the missing evidence from Ryan's case is at the top of that list."

"Missing?" Jana said from the living-room door. "What are you talking about?"

Holly hadn't noticed her sister-in-law's return. Now she waited for Robert to fill his wife in, and when he didn't, she explained in broad terms what she and Matt had discovered.

Jana sent Robert an angry glare. "You knew about this and didn't tell me?"

Ignoring his wife's query, Robert stepped closer to Holly, fury blazing in his eyes. "I told you a long time ago to leave the investigation of Ryan's death to the police. You have no business poking your nose in this!"

Holly met his challenging stare with her own. "I have every right! He was my husband, and I deserve answers!"

Robert quaked with rage, his volume rising. "Leave it alone! You're going to ruin everything!"

Holly jolted. "Ruin everything? What on earth—?"

"Robert? What are you saying?" Jana asked, her face pale.

Biting out a curse, Robert whirled away from Holly and stormed across the room. He hurled his highball glass into the fireplace with a roar.

The first fingers of fear wrapped around Holly's throat. Robert's inebriation made him less predictable, less inhibited, but a need to know the truth pushed her forward. "Did you tamper with the evidence in Ryan's murder?"

Robert said nothing as he glared at her, breathing heavily, his teeth clenched in a snarl.

Jana sank onto the sofa, visibly shaken.

"Were you protecting someone? Covering for someone?" Holly's dread grew as Robert remained silent, glowering darkly from across the room. "Did *you* kill Ryan, Robert?"

Jana gasped.

"No," he growled.

"*Did* you?" Holly shook so hard she could barely stand.

"No!" he shouted.

"Did you set the fire at my house? Did you try to kill *me?*" Her voice trembled, and tears clogged her throat.

Robert snatched up a vase from the mantel and smashed it in the fireplace. "Yes, dammit! I had to stop you, before you ruined everything!"

Horror punched her in the gut. She struggled to draw air into her constricted lungs. "You *did* kill my husband, didn't you?"

"It was an accident!" Robert shouted, tears cracking his voice.

"No!" Jana sobbed, burying her face in her hands.

Holly stared at Robert numbly, too stunned to process more than the fact that she had to leave, had to get away from the man who'd robbed her of the man she had loved. Turning, she staggered toward the door.

"Where are you going?" Robert raged, a note of panic sharpening his tone. "Get back here!"

Holly grabbed her coat and plowed through the front door, not bothering to close it as she rushed to her truck. Through her haze of shock, she heard Robert storm out to the front porch.

"Holly! Get back here! I won't let you ruin me!"

Her hand shook as she fumbled to start her engine. Tears blurred her view as she spun down the driveway.

A tiny voice in her head told her she was too upset to drive, but she couldn't stay and face Robert. Ryan's murderer.

It was an accident!

A fist of grief and disbelief squeezed her throat. She struggled to draw air into her constricted lungs. Blinking hard, she cleared her vision as she hurtled onto the state highway out of town.

Robert had set the fire. Tried to kill her. Matt had been right. Matt...

She reached for her purse on the seat next to her, digging for her cell phone. Keeping one hand on the steering wheel, she thumbed the buttons to call her house.

After several rings, Matt answered, and fresh tears flooded her eyes. She needed his arms around her now, needed him to tell her things would be all right.

"Matt." Her voice cracked.

"Holly? Honey, what's wrong?"

"Robert...killed Ryan. He...said he had to stop me—" She gasped as her tires slid on a patch of ice and the back of her truck fishtailed.

"I'm so sorry, honey. I know this has to be a shock to you."

"Matt, he's family...how could he?" She choked on a sob. Lifting her arm, she wiped her eyes on her coat sleeve.

"Where are you?"

She'd reached the curvy stretch of road that crossed the mountains outside of town. "Coming home. I— Oh God...why didn't I see—"

"Don't, Holly. No one knew."

She drew a fortifying breath, trying to quiet the tempest inside her so she could focus on the road. Glancing in her rearview mirror, she spotted a pair of headlights approaching behind her. Fast.

"Look, we'll talk when you get here," Matt said.

"I have to go. The roads are getting bad and—"

Whomp!

Her truck lurched forward. Holly screamed. Her cell phone flew from her grasp to the floor.

The car behind her had rammed her.

"Holly! Holly, what happened?" Matt's voice filtered through the truck cab from the phone on the passenger-side floor. Out of reach.

Adrenaline coursed through her, spinning her thoughts. She tried to force enough oxygen into her lungs to speak. A check of her mirrors told her the car that had hit her was still riding her bumper.

The idiot! He'd already skidded once on the slick road. Why didn't he back off? Slow down?

"Holly!" She heard panic in Matt's voice.

"I—I'm okay. Someone bumped me from behind."

Grappling to calm herself, Holly cautiously eased off the gas. Bad enough that the dark, twisty road was icing without adding a careless driver to the mix.

With a roar of his engine, the driver behind her gunned his engine and rammed her again.

Intentionally.

Holly gasped. Fought the wheel to keep the truck from spinning off the road. Down the embankment.

"He hit me again!" she cried loud enough for Matt to hear. "On purpose!"

"What?" Matt's voice sounded distant. The mountains were interfering with her connection.

Squeezing the steering wheel, she divided her attention between the bright headlights bearing down on her and the treacherous curves ahead. "The car behind me is ramming me!"

As soon as the words left her mouth, another jarring hit knocked her truck forward. Sliding. Weaving. "Matt!"

Fear rang in Holly's voice.

Matt gripped the phone harder, as if he could reach her, help her by holding the receiver tighter. "Holly? Are you all right? Can you hear me?"

Static buzzed in his ear, then silence. He'd lost her.

He couldn't be sure what was happening to Holly, but he knew something was wrong. She'd hit something. Or something had hit her.

After her scream, he'd had trouble understanding her. But "hit me" had been clear enough. And "Robert killed Ryan."

Robert.

Icy dread skittered through Matt.

Holly was in trouble. He had to get to her. Somehow.

But how? He had no car, no way to—

He jerked his gaze to the brightly lit Christmas tree across the room. The one he'd cut down in the woods with Holly.

And brought back to the farmhouse, towed behind...*her four-wheeler.*

His heart in his throat, Matt ran to the kitchen and snatched the ATV keys from the peg by the back door.

He could only pray he wasn't too late.

Holly battled the skid until her tires found purchase again. Fear strangled her. Panic thrashed in her chest.

Headlights behind her approached again. Shuddering, she stepped on the gas pedal. She couldn't let this crazy run her off the road.

In her peripheral vision, the night-darkened trees and slopes of the mountain terrain flew past with frightening speed. Just as blood rushed past her ears in a deafening whoosh.

Wham!

Holly whimpered as her truck rocked again. The maniac behind her was determined to kill her. She nudged her speed higher, fear climbing her throat as she hurtled around one blind turn after another. Straddling the center line.

Her tires slipped in the packed snow and ice, and her nerves jumped.

If someone came around a curve from the other direction...

She raised a shaking hand to wipe tears from her eyes. She didn't want to crash. Didn't want to die.

Didn't want anyone else hurt because of her.

She couldn't keep up these reckless speeds. She couldn't outrun the homicidal driver behind her. *Robert...*

Somehow she knew that was who was ramming her truck, trying to kill her, even as her brain recoiled at the notion.

Maybe she could talk to him, calm him down....

Wham!

Her Tacoma spun sideways. She yanked the wheel, correcting. Too late. Spinning helplessly, she slid toward the edge of the road. Toward the sheer drop down the side of the mountain.

Matt raced through the frigid night, icy wind lashing him, stinging his eyes as he pushed the all-terrain vehicle to go faster. Faster.

Even with the small headlamp on the ATV, he could barely see the road.

Holly had said she was on her way home. She had to be somewhere along the mountain highway between the farm-house and Morgan Hollow. Between the winter weather and the holiday evening, traffic on the mountain highway was almost nonexistent.

A full moon cast threads of pale light through the evergreens and naked hardwoods that lined the road.

His hands, his face were numb from the wind buffeting his exposed skin. His heart was numb with fear that he could lose another woman he loved.

Robert...said he had to stop me—

A shiver that had nothing to do with the winter night shook him to his core. Matt had no doubt Robert was after Holly.

Robert—who'd killed Ryan.

Matt twisted the throttle, pushed the ATV to go faster. He had to find Holly before Robert had a chance to kill her, too.

With a jarring thump, Holly's truck stopped. The bang of her deploying air bag reverberated through the silent night. Coughing, choking on the dust and fumes from the air bag, she stared through the front window. Into the darkness beyond her front bumper.

White. Snow. She'd struck a snowbank. One of the few places along the highway where the mountain sloped up on this side of the road.

Trembling from head to toe, she leaned her head back and

closed her eyes. She had to have an angel watching out for her. *Ryan*.

When she sucked in a breath, trying to steady her jangling nerves, she gagged on the acrid powder still drifting in the air.

Outside, a car door slammed. She jerked her gaze to her rearview mirror, squinting against the glare of headlights behind her. Backlit by the lights, the dark silhouette of a man strode toward her.

Robert.

A fresh shot of adrenaline streaked through her. Scrambling for her door handle and the latch of her seat belt at the same time, Holly freed herself from the front seat and stumbled from her truck. Her legs quaked so hard she could barely stand.

"Robert!" she shouted, her voice surprisingly strong.

He stopped. Swayed drunkenly. His body blocked one headlamp, allowing her to make out the dark lines of his face, the grim set of his mouth.

Anger and fear tangled in her gut.

"Why are you doing this? You said Ryan's death was an accident. Surely if you explain that to the authorities, you'll get leniency."

He barked a skeptical laugh. "'S too late f'r that."

Robert raised his arm, and in the glare of his car's headlights, she saw the glint of dark metal. His service revolver. Aimed at her.

"Robert, no!" She staggered back, collided with the open door of her truck.

A deafening blast and the shattering of glass ricocheted through the night.

Holly yelped. Ducked. Broken glass from her truck window rained down on her.

"You should have listened to me, Holly! You should have left well enough alone!"

She heard the crunch of snow under Robert's feet. He was closing in.

Holly glanced into her truck. Inside, she'd be a sitting duck.

"If you hadn't started diggin' into Ryan's case, no one would've ever had t' know what happened at th' church. I'd covered m' tracks. Parker had nothin'."

Holly's heart scampered like a trapped rabbit. In a crouch, she scurried around her open truck door, using it as a shield.

"What *did* happen, Robert?" she called. Maybe his drunkenness would loosen his tongue and buy her time. Maybe she still had a chance to reason with him. Maybe all he needed was a chance to soothe his conscience, confess his crime.

A shadow fell over her. Her heart fisting, she glanced up. Robert loomed over her, swaying. His gun now dangled in his hand at his side. His expression was tortured, twisted in grief, guilt and a rage.

Toppling back onto her bottom, hands behind her, Holly sat motionless on the frozen earth. She held her breath, waiting.

"I met him, like he asked, to salv'ge that damn stain'd glass. He wanted to surprise you with it." Robert paused and braced a hand on the Tacoma. "I was late, 'n…he confronted me. About my drinkin'. Said he was worried about Jana and how it'd interfere with me doin' my job." He scoffed. "He threatened me. Said he'd go to the chief of p'lice 'bout me if I didn't quit drinkin', get help." He shook his head and shifted his feet, clearly agitated.

When he waved the gun, Holly tensed.

"He had the nerve to threaten me!" Robert's tone reflected his growing fury. His breathing sawed unevenly, clouding in icy puffs. "We argued. I shoved him. An' he threw a fist."

Holly bit her bottom lip, muffling the whimper of grief that swamped her. Finally, she was learning the truth.

"I grabbed a scrap of wood from th' floor. Swung it. Ryan fell and…didn't get up." Robert's voice broke, and he cleared his throat. "I'm sorry, Holly. I didn't mean to kill 'im. It was an acc'dent. But…I panicked." Robert sighed, scuffed his foot on the icy ground. "I took his watch and shoes, made it look like a mugging. I—"

When he stopped, Holly glanced up in time to see him wipe his face.

Another car passed them on the highway, swinging wide to avoid them, but didn't stop.

Holly's heart sank. "Robert, you...can still make this right. P-put the gun away."

He shook his head. "No. I only told you because...I figured you had a right to know the truth. I've seen how hard the un-answered questions have been on you."

She nodded, praying she could appease him, assuage his guilt. "Thank you...for telling me."

He cocked his head, his expression reflecting an eerie calm. "But...now that you know...I—I can't let you go. Can't let you turn me in. D' you know what would happen to me, a cop, in prison?"

A prickle of alarm bit her spine. "Robert?"

He raised the gun again. And aimed.

"You don't want to hurt me. I know you don't. You swore an oath to protect and serve—"

A flash from the muzzle lit his face for an instant. Distort-ing his features. Making his dark eyes glow with evil intent.

She jerked, her ears ringing, and felt the heat from the bullet as it whizzed past her cheek. Frantic to escape, Holly crab-crawled backward. The ice and gravel at the side of the highway scraped her hands. He fired again. A stinging punch hit her arm, knocking her down. Crying out in pain, she grabbed her arm. Stunned. Terrified.

Robert would kill her if she didn't get out of there.

Gravel danced next to her as Robert squeezed off another shot.

Shoving to her feet, Holly lowered her head—and ran.

Chapter 17

Matt skidded to a stop beside Holly's abandoned truck. Behind it, Robert's car sat empty, the engine still idling. He searched in the dim moonlight for some clue where they could be. The ground below the driver-side door of the Tacoma was littered with broken glass.

And a bullet casing.

Fear kicked Matt's pulse up another notch. He climbed hurriedly to Holly's front seat and opened the glove box. He raked the contents onto the floor until he found what he'd hoped he would. A flashlight. Her cell phone lay on the floor, and he checked the screen. No reception. *Damn.*

Shining the flashlight beam on the snow, he found tracks that led up the mountain slope. He jogged through the calf-deep snow, following the deep footprints. Twenty yards up the incline, he spotted something dark in the snow. He staggered to a stop and dropped to his knees for a better look.

His heart lurched.

The spot was blood.

* * *

Holly clutched her arm, trying to ignore the pain that radiated from her bullet wound with every pounding step. The icy air, the thick snow hampered her progress. She struggled for every frozen breath she drew.

Still, she clambered forward, panting, slipping, clawing her way uphill. When the ground leveled, she wove through the trees, lifting her good arm to block the low hanging branches that slapped at her.

"Holly!"

Robert was close, gaining on her despite his drunkenness. When the ground began sloping down, her feet skidded on the slippery snow. Arms windmilling, she slid several feet down the hill before losing her balance and landing on her bottom. Her breath rushed from her lungs in an "oof."

"Holly, stop!" Robert's voice came from just above her, at the top of the hill.

He fired another shot. Bark splintered from a tree near her. Tears burned her eyes. *I need your help again, Ryan.*

But when she closed her eyes, conjuring an image to give her courage and strength, she saw Matt's face, his warm smile. She didn't want to die tonight. She wanted to spend her life with Matt, wanted to help him regain custody of his children, wanted to have children of their own.

Her hurt and resentment for his lie by omission had blinded her to the simple truth. She wanted a future with the man she loved.

She had to survive this night, Robert's rampage—for Matt.

Gulping a shallow breath, Holly clambered to her feet. She scrambled down the hill, dodging trees and praying.

The crack of gunfire echoed through the woods, and Matt froze. He swung his flashlight in the direction of the noise and squinted into the darkness. "Holly!"

Following the double set of tracks through the woods, he jogged through the snow, wishing the snowy terrain, the weather and visibility allowed him to move faster. Every second counted. Years ago, if he'd gotten home just minutes earlier, he'd have been in time to save Jill. He couldn't bear the thought of being too late to help Holly.

Deeper in the trees, a dark crumpled object appeared in the beam of the flashlight, and he rushed to identify it.

Holly's scarf. Blood stained the fringe.

His pulse spiking, he picked up the neck wrap and jammed it in his jacket pocket. "Holly!"

The footprints led away from where she'd lost the scarf, down a hill, and he set off again. Beyond the illumination of the flashlight, he saw nothing but dark, empty woods.

Holly didn't see the sharp drop in the landscape until too late. She tumbled down the embankment, landing hard on the snow-crusted outcropping some ten to twelve feet below. Winded, she sat up slowly and eyed the edge of the icy rock shelf. Mere feet from where she'd landed, the mountain plunged steeply again. While grateful she hadn't kept sliding and fallen to her death down the sheer escarpment, a quick glance around told her the ledge that had saved her life now trapped her.

The only way off it was back up the embankment she'd fallen down. Climbing the steep wall of icy rock and frozen earth would be tricky at best. Especially with her injured arm. A slippery foothold or crumbled handhold could be disastrous. But what choice did she have?

"Holly!" Robert's voice thundered just above her at the top of the embankment.

Her heart jolted, and she pressed as far back out of his line of sight as possible. Then, with a crack of branches and the whoosh of cascading snow, Robert crashed down the drop-off and onto the outcropping with her.

He staggered to his feet, shaking the snow from his arms—and stumbling dangerously close to the edge.

"Robert, look out!" Holly grabbed the sleeve of his coat and hauled him back.

He snapped his head around and shook free of her hold. "So there…you are," he said, breathless from his pursuit. His arm wavered as he raised the gun again. "No more running."

Stiff from the cold and shock, Holly stumbled back, conscious of how little room she had, how few options to save herself. "Robert, be reasonable. You don't want to kill me. I know you don't. There has to be another way to end this!"

"You think I didn't think about that?" Robert shook his head. "When your friend Randall showed up, I thought I'd found the perfect solution. He had all the makin' of a scapegoat."

A chill slithered through Holly, knowing how she'd bought into Robert's ploy to frame Matt.

"I made sure all the evidence from the fire pointed to him, planted doubts in your head," he boasted. "It was working, too. You believed me."

Guilt sliced Holly to the core. She'd let her hurt feelings and wounded pride blind her to the truth Matt had professed from the beginning. She'd let her doubts drive a wedge between her and Matt.

Now she might never have the chance to apologize to him, to tell him she believed him, that she loved him.

"Robert, if you'll just put the gun down, we can work this out. If you turn yourself in, I'm sure the DA's office will take that into—"

"Turn myself in?" he scoffed. "I told you. I'm not going to prison! I can't! Sorry, Holly. But there's only one way this can end." He steadied the revolver with his other hand and took aim.

Matt heard voices.

Robert.

Holly. Hearing her, knowing she was alive brought a wave of relief crashing over him.

He paused to listen, then moved forward slowly, quietly, following the sounds. As he approached the place where the voices seemed to originate, he flicked off the flashlight and tucked it in the waist of his jeans at the small of his back. Creeping forward, he found Robert and Holly on a narrow ledge below a steep drop of a dozen or so feet. Moonlight peeked through thin clouds, casting the scene in a surreal glow.

Robert had Holly cornered, backed to the end of the ledge. At the business end of his service weapon.

Ice streaked through Matt's blood. He watched in horror as Robert leveled and steadied the gun.

Matt's time had run out. He raced to the embankment. Jumped.

He landed on Robert's back, and the momentum of his fall knocked Robert off his feet. Grappling with Robert in the snow, he fought to immobilize Robert's arms and legs. Pin him to the frozen ground.

But Robert fought back with skill and strength and determination. He wrestled an arm free and lobbed a punch to Matt's jaw that stunned him long enough for Robert to twist free and clamber to his feet.

For a few precious seconds, Holly stared in disbelief as the two men writhed in the snow, battling for the upper hand.

Matt. As if conjured by her prayers, the deepest desire of her heart, he was there. But her relief quickly turned to a stark fear as the men rolled near the edge of the cliff.

Then she saw it. In the snow, just over a yard from her feet. Hovering at the edge of the icy rock outcropping.

Robert's gun.

Matt's tackle or the impact of Robert's fall had knocked the weapon from her brother-in-law's hands.

But as she edged toward the revolver, Robert struggled free

of Matt's grip and shoved to his feet. Turning, Robert narrowed a menacing look on her, followed the line of her gaze.

And lunged for the gun.

The weapon skittered over the edge, clattering on the rocks below.

Landing on his back, Robert slid on the ice and scrambled to find traction. Holly gasped as his feet skidded off the edge, flailing over the sharp drop to the valley below.

"Robert!" she screamed.

In a blur of motion, Matt dove toward Robert. He grabbed for Robert's coat, but only caught the hood. The snap-on hood pulled free of the coat, but in the split second that Matt's grab slowed Robert's fall, her brother-in-law snagged hold of Matt's sleeve.

Robert's weight jerked Matt to the rim of the icy ledge.

"No!" Holly's strangled cry echoed off the trees, reverberating in the cold winter night.

With all his strength, Matt planted the palm of his hand on the icy ledge, caught a ridge of rock and braced. Prayed.

He slid a few more inches before stopping, hovering over the edge of the abyss. He peered down, into Robert's panicked eyes.

"Hold on!" he gritted through clenched teeth. "I'll pull you up."

Matt took a second to assess the situation. With the slightest move, he could lose his handhold and careen over the edge with Robert.

"Matt!" Holly crawled toward him, her own feet skidding and scrambling on the slick ice and snow.

"Get back! It's too dangerous." The last thing he needed was Holly risking her neck to rescue him and falling to her death.

She ignored him. Dropping to her bottom, she grabbed his legs and braced her heels to keep him from sliding farther toward the edge.

"Randall," Robert rasped.

Matt found the man's gaze again. But Robert's expression was different.

Calmer. Peaceful. Resigned.

"Tell Jana I'm sorry."

A tingle of premonition prickled Matt's nape.

And Robert let go.

Holly sucked in a sharp, sobbing breath. "Oh, God."

Free of Robert's weight, Matt used his handhold to push safely back from the ledge. He pulled the flashlight from the waist of his jeans and, easing forward, shone the beam into the crevasse below.

The unnatural angle of Robert's neck attested that he hadn't survived the fall. With a sigh, Matt snapped off the flashlight and scooted safely back from the edge.

"Is he—?" Holly's voice warbled, and he carefully drew her into his arms.

"I'm sorry." He absorbed the shudder that raced through her and squeezed her tighter. When she winced, he remembered the blood he'd seen. He jerked back, scanning her for injury. "I found blood in the snow. Where are you hurt—?"

She tugged at her sleeve. "My arm. It hurts, but I don't think it's dcep."

After helping her peel her coat off her shoulder, he flicked the flashlight back on to examine her wound, while her gaze drifted back toward the drop-off. She drew a quivering breath. "How do I tell Jana? Losing Robert will be hard enough for her without knowing what he did, how he—" She swiped at tears, beading on her cheeks. "He killed Ryan. By accident. But then he covered it up and—tried to frame you."

Matt raised his gaze to meet hers. "The truth will be hard for her to hear, but…you know better than anyone that healing can only start when you know the truth."

She nodded, and he pressed a kiss to her forehead.

As she'd thought, Holly had no more than a flesh wound, though she'd need stitches to close the gash. He dug in his pocket for her scarf and, his hands numb from the cold and shaking from post-adrenaline aftermath, wound it around her arm to staunch the bleeding. "When I heard that gunshot, I was so scared, Holly. Terrified that I was too late again. That I'd lost another woman I loved, because I hadn't been there when you needed me—"

Emotion rose in his throat to choke him, and she cupped his cheek with a cold hand.

"You've been there *every time* I needed you. You've saved my life twice and…you've given me a reason to be happy again."

Matt's breath stalled in his lungs. He searched her tearful gaze in the shimmer of moonlight. "I don't know if I can ever forgive myself for hurting you."

Wrinkling her nose and tilting her head, she drilled a piercing gaze on him. "Well, that's a problem then. Because I forgive you. And I was hoping we could start over…with a clean slate."

Matt's heart clenched, and he struggled for the breath to answer. "Hi. I'm Matt Randall. I'm a pediatrician. A widower. Father of two wonderful kids." He sucked in a ragged breath and smiled. "And I love you, Holly."

Rising on her toes, she pressed a warm kiss to his lips. "I love you, too. So much."

Epilogue

Christmas Eve—One year later

"**Y**ou look beautiful, Holly Noel." Standing in the narthex of the Morgan Hollow Methodist Church as the pre-wedding music signaled the ceremony was ready to start, Neil Bancroft brushed a kiss on his middle daughter's cheek and beamed at her proudly. "Are you sure Matt can't set up his medical clinic in Lagniappe? I'd underwrite it, if it meant having my girl back home."

Holly twisted her lips in a crooked grin. "Thank you, Dad. But I've told you, Morgan Hollow is my home now. And getting the grant for the new clinic is a big deal for Matt, a new beginning. This is where we belong."

Neil pressed his lips in a taut line of resignation and nodded. "I just hate that my girls are all leaving the nest." He sighed and glanced to the door of the sanctuary where Zoey and Paige were queued to walk down the aisle. "First you, now Zoey's off roaming the country with that bum—"

"Dad," Holly scolded, "you promised."

He gave her an apologetic grin. "Well, at least Paige and Brent will be close by after they marry. One out of three is better than nothing."

The organ played the first notes of the processional, and Holly's pulse kicked. She gave one last worried glance toward the front door of the church. Her specially invited guests hadn't shown. Shoving aside her disappointment, she looped her arm through her father's. "I think that's our cue."

Paige waved Holly over impatiently. "Come on, Hol. It's time!"

"Like they can start without her," Zoey said. "Chill, sis."

Holly grinned at her sisters, so opposite in personality yet both stunning in their Christmas green dresses. Beyond choosing Christmas Eve for the wedding, Holly had picked the dress color knowing it would complement both Zoey's auburn hair and Paige's raven tresses.

Holly took a deep breath as she watched her sisters take their place at the front of the church, then hugged her father's arm tightly as they started down the aisle. Only then did she steal a glimpse of her groom.

Matt met her eyes, and the smile he sent her said so much. She read the depth of his love, the breadth of his happiness—and the hole in his heart, not having his children with him to share this day.

Her heart ached for Matt, despite all the happiness they'd found together and the progress he'd made toward opening the new health clinic at the Community Aid Center.

As she passed Jana, her sister-in-law gave her a bittersweet smile. The year had been rough for Jana, but she was healing, even dating again.

With a final peck on the cheek from her father, Holly took her place beside Matt and laced her fingers with his.

"Happy birthday," he whispered.

She blinked and grinned broadly. "With all the wedding events, I almost forgot."

"Dearly beloved, we are gathered here to witness the marriage of Holly and Matthew," the minister began, and Matt squeezed her fingers. "Marriage is a sacred union—"

The crash of the narthex door interrupted the minister, and Holly jerked her gaze to the back of the church, hoping...praying.

An older couple with two small children stood at the end of the middle aisle, glancing awkwardly about for a seat. Beside her, Holly felt Matt stiffen, draw a shaky breath.

The older child, a girl, gasped as she looked toward the altar rail. "Daddy!"

Matt dropped Holly's hand and ran to swoop his daughter into his arms. "Palmer! Oh, God, I've missed you!" The emotion in Matt's voice, the tears of joy streaming down his cheeks were the best wedding present, the best Christmas present Holly could have asked for.

Clutching Palmer in his arms, he strode over to Jill's parents and gathered Miles into his embrace as well. "Thank you," he told them hoarsely.

Jill's mother cleared her throat. "Thank your bride. She's the one who convinced us it was time to put hard feelings behind us and do what was right for Palmer and Miles. We're returning custody to you and your new wife...if you'll promise us visitation rights."

Matt shot a look of stunned disbelief to Holly before nodding to his in-laws. "Of course. Any time you want."

A happy murmur rippled through the congregation as more hugs were exchanged and Matt kissed both of his children's heads over and over again.

Holly waited patiently at the altar, tears streaking her makeup and her heart bursting with joy as she watched Matt's reunion with his children.

Finally, Zoey called to the back of the church, "Hey, Matt, did you forget something? Say...your wedding?"

Matt laughed with the congregation and, one child in each arm, he marched back to the front of the church. Paige and Zoey each claimed one of Matt's kids to hold as he turned back to Holly, wiping his wet cheeks with his palms.

He tugged Holly close and captured her face between his hands. "You did this?" he whispered, his blue eyes bright with moisture and jubilance.

She nodded, whispering back. "I've been in touch with Jill's folks off and on for months, working toward a compromise, convincing them to give you a chance."

"But you never said anything to me—"

"Because I didn't know if I could change their minds. You'd been trying for years without luck, and until they walked into the church, I wasn't sure what they'd decided about custody."

Matt looked past her to his children again, his expression stunned—but happier than she'd ever seen him. When his gaze shifted back to her, the love in his eyes flooded her with warmth and joy. "I have everything now. Because of you. How can I ever thank you?"

She flashed him an impish grin. "Marry me?"

Matt laughed and turned to the minister. "I think we're ready now."

Holly clung tightly to Matt's hands as they exchanged promises of forever love and faithfulness, and when the minister pronounced them man, wife...*and family,* Palmer and Miles rushed forward to join them.

With his children bouncing excitedly beside him, Matt drew Holly close and sealed with a kiss the vows he'd made to his Christmas bride.

* * * * *

The Bancroft Brides continues in 2010 when
Holly's sisters get their own shot at happily-ever-after.
Coming soon from Beth Cornelison and
Silhouette Romantic Suspense!

*Celebrate 60 years of pure reading pleasure
with Harlequin®!*

To commemorate the event, Silhouette Special Edition
invites you to Ashley O'Ballivan's bed-and-breakfast in
the small town of Stone Creek. The beautiful innkeeper
will have her hands full caring for her old flame Jack
McCall. He's on the run and recovering from a mysteri-
ous illness, but that won't stop him from trying to win
Ashley back.

*Enjoy an exclusive glimpse of Linda Lael Miller's
AT HOME IN STONE CREEK
Available in November 2009 from
Silhouette Special Edition®*

The helicopter swung abruptly sideways in a dizzying arch, setting Jack McCall's fever-ravaged brain spinning.

His friend's voice sounded tinny, coming through the earphones. "You belong in a hospital," he said. "Not some backwater bed-and-breakfast."

All Jack really knew about the virus raging through his system was that it wasn't contagious, and there was no known treatment for it besides a lot of rest and quiet. "I don't like hospitals," he responded, hoping he sounded like his normal self. "They're full of sick people."

Vince Griffin chuckled but it was a dry sound, rough at the edges. "What's in Stone Creek, Arizona?" he asked. "Besides a whole lot of nothin'?"

Ashley O'Ballivan was in Stone Creek, and she was a whole lot of somethin', but Jack had neither the strength nor the inclination to explain. After the way he'd ducked out six months before, he didn't expect a welcome, knew he didn't deserve one.

But Ashley, being Ashley, would take him in whatever her misgivings.

He had to get to Ashley; he'd be all right.

He closed his eyes, letting the fever swallow him.

There was no telling how much time had passed when he became aware of the chopper blades slowing overhead. Dimly, he saw the private ambulance waiting on the airfield outside of Stone Creek; it seemed that twilight had descended.

Jack sighed with relief. His clothes felt clammy against his flesh. His teeth began to chatter as two figures unloaded a gurney from the back of the ambulance and waited for the blades to stop.

"Great," Vince remarked, unsnapping his seat belt. "Those two look like volunteers, not real EMTs."

The chopper bounced sickeningly on its runners, and Vince, with a shake of his head, pushed open his door and jumped to the ground, head down.

Jack waited, wondering if he'd be able to stand on his own. After fumbling unsuccessfully with the buckle on his seat belt, he decided not.

When it was safe the EMTs approached, following Vince, who opened Jack's door.

His old friend Tanner Quinn stepped around Vince, his grin not quite reaching his eyes.

"You look like hell warmed over," he told Jack cheerfully.

"Since when are you an EMT?" Jack retorted.

Tanner reached in, wedged a shoulder under Jack's right arm and hauled him out of the chopper. His knees immediately buckled, and Vince stepped up, supporting him on the other side.

"In a place like Stone Creek," Tanner replied, "everybody helps out."

They reached the wheeled gurney, and Jack found himself on his back.

Tanner and the second man strapped him down, a process that brought back a few bad memories.

"Is there even a hospital in this place?" Vince asked irritably from somewhere in the night.

"There's a pretty good clinic over in Indian Rock," Tanner answered easily, "and it isn't far to Flagstaff." He paused to help his buddy hoist Jack and the gurney into the back of the ambulance. "You're in good hands, Jack. My wife is the best veterinarian in the state."

Jack laughed raggedly at that.

Vince muttered a curse.

Tanner climbed into the back beside him, perched on some kind of fold-down seat. The other man shut the doors.

"You in any pain?" Tanner said as his partner climbed into the driver's seat and started the engine.

"No." Jack looked up at his oldest and closest friend and wished he'd listened to Vince. Ever since he'd come down with the virus—a week after snatching a five-year-old girl back from her non-custodial parent, a small-time Colombian drug dealer—he hadn't been able to think about anyone or anything but Ashley. When he *could* think, anyway.

Now, in one of the first clearheaded moments he'd experienced since checking himself out of Bethesda the day before, he realized he might be making a major mistake. Not by facing Ashley—he owed her that much and a lot more. No, he could be putting her in danger, putting Tanner and his daughter and his pregnant wife in danger, too.

"I shouldn't have come here," he said, keeping his voice low.

Tanner shook his head, his jaw clamped down hard as though he was irritated by Jack's statement.

"This is where you belong," Tanner insisted. "If you'd had sense enough to know that six months ago, old buddy, when you bailed on Ashley without so much as a fare-thee-well, you wouldn't be in this mess."

Ashley. The name had run through his mind a million times in those six months, but hearing somebody say it out loud was like having a fist close around his insides and squeeze hard.

Jack couldn't speak.

Tanner didn't press for further conversation.

The ambulance bumped over country roads, finally hitting smooth blacktop.

"Here we are," Tanner said. "Ashley's place."

* * * * *

Will Jack be able to patch things up with Ashley,
or will his past put the woman he loves in harm's way?
Find out in
AT HOME IN STONE CREEK
by Linda Lael Miller
Available November 2009 from
Silhouette Special Edition®

NEW YORK TIMES BESTSELLING AUTHOR

SHARON SALA

THE DAUGHTER OF A FORBIDDEN LOVE COMES HOME....

As a legacy of hatred erupts in a shattering moment of violence, a dying mother entrusts her newborn daughter to a caring stranger. Now, twenty-five years later, Katherine Fane has come home to Camarune, Kentucky, to bury the woman who'd raised her, bringing a blood feud to its searing conclusion.

At the cabin in the woods where she was born, Katherine is drawn to the ravaged town and its violent past. But her arrival has not gone unnoticed. A stranger is watching from the woods, a shattered old man is witnessing the impossible, and Sheriff Luke DePriest's only thoughts are to keep Katherine safe from the sleeping past she has unwittingly awoken....

THE RETURN

Available September 29, 2009, wherever books are sold!

MIRA®

MSS2677

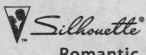

Silhouette®

Romantic
SUSPENSE

**Sparked by Danger,
Fueled by Passion.**

*Blackout
At Christmas*

Beth Cornelison,
Sharron McClellan,
Jennifer Morey

What happens when a major blackout shuts
down the entire Western seaboard on Christmas
Eve? Follow stories of danger, intrigue and
romance as three women learn to trust their
instincts to survive and open their hearts to the
love that unexpectedly comes their way.

*Available November
wherever books are sold.*

Visit Silhouette Books at www.eHarlequin.com

SRS27653

HARLEQUIN® *Blaze*™

Once upon a time...

There was a young, overworked fairy godmother who wanted to experience life, love—and most of all, desire!

And there was also a long-lost princess who came home to claim her crown. Only, she decided to run away with the big bad wolf instead.

Luckily, they both lived sexily ever after!

Let bestselling authors Julie Leto and Leslie Kelly tell you a bedtime story that will inspire you to do anything but sleep!

Pick up

More Blazing Bedtime Stories

Available November 2009

Fairy tales have never been so hot!

---

red-hot reads

nocturne™

TIME RAIDERS
THE PROTECTOR

by *USA TODAY* bestselling author
MERLINE LOVELACE

Former USAF officer Cassandra Jones's unique psychic skills come in handy, as she has been selected to join the elite Time Raiders squad. Her first mission is to travel back to seventh-century China to locate the final piece of a missing bronze medallion. Major Max Brody is assigned to accompany her, and soon Cassandra and Max have to fight their growing attraction to each other while the mission suddenly turns deadly....

Available November
wherever books are sold.

SN61822

Silhouette®

Romantic

SUSPENSE

COMING NEXT MONTH

Available October 27, 2009

#1583 BLACKOUT AT CHRISTMAS
"Stranded with the Bridesmaid" by Beth Cornelison
"Santa Under Cover" by Sharron McClellan
"Kiss Me on Christmas" by Jennifer Morey
In these short stories, three couples find themselves stranded in a
city-wide blackout during a Christmas Eve blizzard.

#1584 THE COWBODY'S SECRET TWINS—Carla Cassidy
Top Secret Deliveries
All Henry Randolf wants for Christmas is to be left alone. But
Melissa Morgan shows up at his Texas ranch with adorable twin boys—
quite clearly *his* twin boys—and he knows his life will never be the same.
When a crazed killer puts the new family in his sights, Henry and Melissa
must learn to work together—for their love and for the safety of their boys.

#1585 HIS WANTED WOMAN—Linda Turner
The O'Reilly Brothers
As a special agent, Patrick O'Reilly always has to put duty before desire.
But his current suspect, Mackenzie Sloan, is tempting him beyond belief.
Her eyes assert her innocence, though the evidence is against her. Will
Patrick decide to trust his head…or his heart?

#1586 IMMINENT AFFAIR—Sheri WhiteFeather
Warrior Society
The first time warrior Daniel Deer Runner met Allie Whirlwind, he
was injured saving her life. Now there are gaps in Daniel's memory—
a memory that includes falling in love with Allie. But when Allie's in
danger again, he's hell-bent on protecting her. Will their old feelings
resurface before time runs out?